LANTERN SAM

and the *BLUE STREAK BANDITS*

Also by
MICHAEL D. BEIL

Summer at Forsaken Lake

The Red Blazer Girls: The Ring of Rocamadour

The Red Blazer Girls: The Vanishing Violin

The Red Blazer Girls: The Mistaken Masterpiece

The Red Blazer Girls: The Secret Cellar

LANTERN SAM
and the *BLUE STREAK BANDITS*

Michael D. Beil

A YEARLING BOOK

Text copyright © 2014 by Michael D. Beil
Cover art and interior illustrations copyright © 2014 by Roman Muradov

All rights reserved. Published in the United States by Yearling, an imprint of Random House Children's Books, a division of Penguin Random House LLC, New York. Originally published in hardcover in the United States by Alfred A. Knopf, an imprint of Random House Children's Books, New York, in 2014.

Yearling and the jumping horse design are registered trademarks of Penguin Random House LLC.

Visit us on the Web! randomhousekids.com
Educators and librarians, for a variety of teaching tools, visit us at RHTeachersLibrarians.com

The Library of Congress has cataloged the hardcover edition of this work as follows:
Beil, Michael D.
Lantern Sam and the Blue Streak bandits / Michael D. Beil.—First edition.
p. cm.
Summary: In 1938, eleven-year-old Henry Shipley must rely on a talking cat named Lantern Sam and a kindly conductor named Clarence to help solve the kidnapping of a young heiress aboard the Lake Erie Shoreliner passenger train.
ISBN 978-0-385-75317-3 (trade) — ISBN 978-0-385-75318-0 (lib. bdg.) — ISBN 978-0-385-75319-7 (ebook)
[1. Railroad trains—Fiction. 2. Cats—Fiction. 3. Human-animal communication—Fiction. 4. Kidnapping—Fiction. 5. Mystery and detective stories.] I. Title.
PZ7.B38823495Lan 2014
[Fic]—dc23
2013013509

ISBN 978-0-385-75320-3 (pbk.)

Printed in the United States of America
10 9 8 7 6 5 4 3 2 1
First Yearling Edition 2015

To Stephen Eric

Chapter 1

The first time I saw Clarence Nockwood, the conductor aboard the Lake Erie Shoreliner, he was standing on the green-carpeted platform of New York's Grand Central Terminal, adjusting the hands of his pocket watch. When he was satisfied that it matched the time shown on the station clock *exactly*, he looked up to see my mother, baby sister, and me in a desperate race against that clock to catch his train. Clarence was very particular about his Elgin watch, and some might say that he was obsessed with punctuality, but to him, being on time was a matter of pride. The Shoreliner, one of the famous express trains of the 1930s and '40s that carried passengers in under twenty hours from New York to Chicago—a distance of 960 miles—was never as fast, famous, or luxurious as the

Twentieth Century Limited or the Broadway Limited, but it *was* well known for being on time. If the departure was scheduled for one-seventeen, the Shoreliner departed at one-seventeen—"on the dot," as Clarence would say.

"All aboard!" cried Clarence as he slipped his watch into his vest pocket. "Lake Erie Shoreliner for Chicago! First stop, Albany! All aboard!"

My mother, dressed in a simple but stylish suit and modest heels, was running as fast as she could down the platform toward him, with my two-year-old sister, Jessica, cradled in one arm and a small suitcase in her other hand. A few steps behind them, I struggled to keep up, wrestling with a piece of luggage nearly twice my size.

"Wait, wait for us!" Mother shouted.

Grinning, Clarence helped us aboard and instructed a porter to help with our bags.

"Thank you . . . thank you," Mother managed to say between breaths. "I thought for sure we'd missed it."

Clarence checked the time on his pocket watch again and smiled at her. "Made it with thirty seconds to spare. You folks going to Chicago?"

"We're going home to Ashtabula. My dad is the captain of a ship, the *Point Pelee*," I bragged. "Have you ever heard of it?"

"I'm afraid not," admitted Clarence. "I don't know much

about boats and such. But if you want to know anything about trains, I'm your man."

"It's not a boat; it's a *ship*," I said. Knowing the difference between boats and ships was *serious* business in the Shipley household.

"And I'm sure it's a fine ship, too. Now, if you'll excuse me a second. Hold on, folks. Here we go!" announced Clarence, and at exactly seventeen minutes past one on May 22, 1938, the Lake Erie Shoreliner chugged out of Grand Central Terminal in New York City and began to snake its way north along the Hudson River.

The Great Depression was still going strong in 1938, but the Shipley family was "making do," as Mother was fond of saying. We were more fortunate than most because Father—Captain Charles Shipley, that is—still had his job, but as a ship's captain he was away at sea for weeks, and sometimes months, at a time. Normally, we would not have been able to afford a train trip to New York City, but Mother had recently inherited a small amount of money and a few pieces of not-very-valuable jewelry from a distant relative who lived there, and the relative's lawyer, a fussy little man whose suit smelled of coffee and burnt toast, had insisted that she travel to New York in person to pick it up and sign the necessary papers. And so, Mother, Jessica, and I made the trip without Father, whose ship was, at that very moment, steaming east past the Colchester Reef lighthouse in western Lake Erie.

Unlike the Twentieth Century Limited, the Shoreliner wasn't quite an "all-sleeper" train. There were a few coach seats available near the onboard barbershop at the back of the club car, but Mother had decided to splurge (just a little), buying "section" tickets. They weren't as comfortable or as private as a drawing room, but they were much less expensive.

"You never know when we might need that extra money," she explained as we settled into our seats. "I know it's a little snug, but it's only for a little while. We'll be back home before you know it, and you'll get to sleep in your own bed later tonight."

"Can I go back to the observation car?" I asked. "I want to watch the boats on the river."

"Just be careful. Promise? Why don't you take your new sketchbook and draw me a picture? Here, take this, in case you want to buy something to drink." She handed me a nickel, which I tucked deep into my front pocket. "And make sure you're back here in time for dinner. I'm going to treat you to a special meal tonight."

Until my sister came along, I had been an only child for eight years, so I was used to entertaining myself. I started out by wandering forward and peeking inside the combination mail and baggage car, which was directly behind the locomotive. A young porter bumped into me as I stood there wondering how I could get into the cab of the locomotive.

"You lost, young fella? Everything's back thataway," he said, pointing over my shoulder. "Just mail and baggage up here."

"Oh. Thanks," I said, sneaking one last peek into the car before turning around and heading down the narrow passageway of the two 8-1-2 sleeper cars at the front of the train. Like all sleeper cars, they got their name from the way they were set up. In this case, there were eight sections, one drawing room, and two compartments in each car. Our section was in the second of the two cars, and the curtain was still open when I went past. Mother didn't notice—her nose was already buried in *Gone with the Wind*, which she had borrowed from the Ashtabula library before our trip and was reading for the second time in less than two weeks.

Next came the dining car, its tables all set with glistening china, crystal, and silver, waiting for the dinner crowd. As I left that scene behind, I stepped into the vestibule of the first of three roomette cars, and paused to admire the view down the shoulder-width hallway that seemed to go on forever. Each car had twenty-two doors leading to twenty-two ingeniously designed miniature rooms, and after walking past sixty-six doors, I stepped into the bright lights of the club car. Although we were barely out of the station, it was already bustling, with all but two of the shiny leather seats filled and the bartender busy shaking drinks. The air was blue with cigarette smoke as men and women sipped cocktails, chatting and laughing noisily, and ignored me completely. It was my first time in a bar, and I lingered for a few minutes, mesmerized, before ducking into the winding passages of the three 4-4-2 sleeper cars, where the more well-to-do travelers were likely to be found. (The four bedrooms, four compartments, and two drawing rooms were different widths, giving the hallway twists and turns.)

And finally, at the back, where the caboose would be on a freight train, was the observation car. In addition to the observation area and lounge, it also contained the Commodore Perry suite—the most expensive accommodations on the Shoreliner. I roamed all the way to the rear of the car, past businessmen who glanced over their newspapers at me and excited young couples marveling at the sights of the city, and dropped myself into a backward-facing seat where I could watch the Hudson slide by as the train accelerated, rocking gently on the tracks.

In the weeks before the trip to New York, I had saved up a few pennies, and at the first newsstand I found, I bought the latest copies of my favorite comic books—*The Shadow* and *Dick Tracy*, along with a new one, *Tailspin Tommy.* I didn't tell Mother (even though it was my money, I just couldn't bear the thought of the disappointed look on her face when she saw what I had chosen to spend it on) and stuck them inside the cover of my sketchbook, saving them for a quiet, relaxing time when I could sit back and really *savor* every word and colored panel without feeling guilty.

Before I even had a chance to discover what evil lurked in the hearts of men, though, a tugboat towing a barge up the river caught my attention, so I fished a stub of pencil out of my shirt pocket and opened my sketchpad. I leafed past the drawings of the Manhattan skyscrapers I had made from our hotel room on Fifty-First Street and stopped at a clean sheet. Working quickly as the train rumbled north, I rough-sketched the scene, managing to get just the outline of the tugboat and a few details down before the train tracks followed a bend in the river and the scene disappeared from view.

"Hey, that's pretty good," said an unfamiliar voice. A *girl's* voice.

I spun around and there she was, leaning over my seat, spying on me. Instinctively, I closed my sketchbook. I didn't like showing my drawings to anyone, especially not to nosy girls I didn't even know.

She pointed out the window as the train went around another bend, bringing the tugboat back into view. "Look! You can see it again. Open up your sketchbook! Hurry!"

But I just stared at her, gripping the pad tightly in my hand just in case she had some idea of snatching it from me. Girls are like that.

"What's the matter? Don't you want to draw anymore? You're really *quite* talented. I peeked at the drawings you made of the city. Don't you just *love* New York? I can't imagine living anywhere else. We live on Fifth Avenue, right across from Central Park. Did you ever visit the park? You really should have, you know. Did you know that it's more than eight hundred acres?"

I'm pretty sure my jaw was hanging open as I listened to the girl, who had obviously been spying on me from the moment I'd sat down.

"Do you always spy on people?" I asked when she finally took a breath. "My mother says that's rude."

The girl grinned at me, and her eyes, which perfectly matched her emerald-green cotton jumper, twinkled mischievously behind the mop of dark curls that framed her face. "So does mine. But I don't care. I can't help it if I want to *know* about people. How are you supposed to learn about them if you don't pay attention to them? *Close* attention."

I didn't know how to answer that. One thing I knew for sure: she wasn't like any of the girls back home in Ashtabula.

While I sat there not saying a word, the girl kept right on talking, so fast that I had trouble keeping up. "I was the first one aboard, and I watched *everyone* else get on," she said. "We're staying in the Commodore Perry suite at the front of this car. We usually take the Twentieth Century Limited when we go to Chicago. It's *so* much more luxurious, don't you think?" Unfazed by my silence, she took a breath and continued. "I remember you—you were the last one to board, thirty seconds before departure time. Mother says I have a photographic memory. You were with your mother and your baby sister. Your mother was wearing a green dress and a black coat. And a hat with a purple—well, more like lavender, actually—flower on the left side. I'm Ellie, by the way. Ellie Strasbourg, like the city in France. Last month, I turned one whole decade old. What's your name? Wait, let me guess . . . it's . . . Herbert."

"No!"

"Woodrow?"

"No."

"Calvin?"

"No. It's Henry," I answered before she tried Grover or Abraham or Chester, or some other president's name.

"Henry what?"

"Henry Shipley. That was my great-grandfather's name, too."

She reached her hand over the seat to shake mine. "Hi, Henry Shipley. It is a pleasure to make your acquaintance." As I looked around the car uncomfortably, certain that everyone was watching and laughing at me, she did just about the worst thing I could have imagined: she abandoned her seat and took the one next to me. "Where are you going?" she asked as I stood to leave, still gripping my sketchpad. I had to get out of there before she did something *really* embarrassing.

"I, um, have to go," I mumbled.

"Don't be silly," she said. "We're on a train. Where could you possibly have to go? I just want someone to talk to. I'm not going to bite you. Although Father says that I may *talk* someone to death one day. Isn't that just the funniest thing ever? The only other children on this train are much too young to be interesting, so I'm afraid you're stuck with me—at least until Erie. That's where we're getting off.

We're going to Conneaut Lake Park to ride the Blue Streak. Have you heard of it?"

I sat back down, suddenly impressed. Of *course* I had heard of the Blue Streak. Every kid for miles around had heard of it and dreamed of riding it. It was the newest, biggest, fastest, and scariest roller coaster in the whole country, and its grand opening was scheduled for May 23, the very next day.

"You're taking the train all the way from New York just to ride the Blue Streak? Boy, you're lucky. I doubt if I'll *ever* get to ride it, and I only live a few miles away. Mother says amusement parks are a waste of money."

"Oh. Sorry. I hope I didn't sound like I was bragging. It's—my daddy is friends with Mr. Vettel, the man who designed it, and he invited us. I know—I'll ask him if you can come, too!"

"I don't think so. My parents would never let me go. And besides, my father is coming home tonight. He's been away on his ship for weeks."

"Is he an explorer?" Ellie asked. "Like Sir Francis Drake? Or Robert Peary? We learned about them in school. Don't you just *love* learning about history?"

Not especially, I thought, suddenly picturing myself staring at the clock in history class, willing the hands to move faster. "He's not an explorer; he's the captain of a ship that carries iron ore, the *Point Pelee*. I'd rather learn about science any day. I'm going to be a naval architect and design the biggest, fastest, and best ships ever. You have to know lots about science to do that."

Ellie hopped up and down in her seat. "You can come to New York and work for my daddy! He *builds* ships! It will be so much fun!"

"I don't know . . . it takes a long time to learn everything you need to know. I have to go to college first, and then . . ."

"I'm going to be a famous detective," said Ellie. "Just like Nancy Drew. Have you read any of her stories? No, I don't suppose you have. Mother says it's not a proper occupation for a lady, but I don't care."

As if I weren't uncomfortable enough with the idea of sitting next to a girl I barely knew, she leaned even closer to me. "Do you want to know a secret?" Without waiting for a response, she continued, whispering, "There are *criminals* aboard this train."

I felt my eyes widen. I had to admit to myself that she was getting a lot more interesting—for a girl.

"I thought that might get your attention," she said.

"How do you know they're criminals?"

"Simple. I recognized them from their pictures. Every Friday the post office puts up new pictures of the FBI's most-wanted criminals, and I go every week to study them. The only problem is, I can't remember their names. I'm better with pictures than words."

It took a second for that all to sink in. Had she really just said that she went to the post office every week to study the Most Wanted posters? I glanced down at my sketchbook to make sure she couldn't see the comic books.

"What are you going to do?" I asked.

"I'm keeping an eye on them, or I was, until I lost them. They must have gone into their compartment. I'll bet they're planning something, because they were acting very suspiciously. Before the train left New York, they were talking with someone I couldn't see on the platform. They tried to hide behind a baggage cart, but I saw them."

"You think they're going to rob the train?" At least that would make the trip a little more exciting, I thought.

"I don't know. Yet, that is. That's what *we're* going to find out."

"*We're?*"

"You *do* want to help me, don't you?"

"I—I don't know," I stammered. "My mom wouldn't like it—"

"Just think of it. We could be famous," said Ellie. "Like Dick Tracy. Or the Shadow."

Oh, that's just swell—she must have seen my comics!

"Maybe you should tell the conductor instead," I said.

"What should you tell me?" asked Clarence the Conductor, who had approached us from behind without our noticing. "Is something wrong?"

Our gasps were followed by sighs of relief as we both spun around to see the conductor's kindly face gazing down at us.

"Oh—you scared me!" said Ellie. "I didn't even hear you come into the car."

"Sorry, miss—didn't mean to frighten you. Was there something you two wanted to tell me?"

I looked at Ellie, who shook her head ever so slightly, and then up at Clarence. "No, sir. We were just . . . playing a little game, that's all."

Clarence, who seemed to know that I wasn't telling the whole truth, didn't push the matter any further. "Is this your first time aboard the Shoreliner?" When I nodded, he checked his pocket watch. "How would you kids like to meet a good friend of mine? I'll take you on a little tour of the train, too. My name is Clarence, by the way. Clarence Nockwood. I'm the head conductor."

Ellie jumped to her feet. "I'm Ellie, and this is Henry, and we would *love* to take a tour of the train. Can we see the kitchen? I always wanted to see inside a train kitchen."

"Don't see why not," said Clarence. "Follow me."

He gave us what he called the "nickel tour" (at the end, I was relieved to learn that it wasn't *literally* a nickel tour, and the money Mother had given me remained safe in my pocket), leading us back up the long passageways and allowing us to poke our heads into an empty roomette. When we got to the dining car, he squeezed us through the cramped, steamy kitchen, where the chef—busy preparing for the dinner service—smiled at Ellie and me, handing us each a freshly baked dinner roll, still warm from the oven. Then Clarence led us to the car at the front of the train— the one that I had peeked into during my self-guided tour. In addition to the baggage and mail, that car also contained the dormitory compartment where all the conductors, por- ters, cooks, and other train workers took their breaks and slept when they were off duty. Clarence pulled the curtain of his private section back, and a long, lean calico cat slowly lifted his head from the bed and looked up at our surprised faces.

"Mrrrraaaaaa," he said.

"Kids, meet my old friend Lantern Sam," said Clarence. "Sorry to interrupt your deep-thinking session, big fella, but I want you to meet some new friends, Ellie and Henry. Sam's been with me on the Shoreliner for going on five years now. Used to ride the freight trains, but decided that the food's better and the beds are more comfortable on passenger trains."

"Lantern Sam—that's a funny name," Ellie said. "Can I pet her?"

"Absolutely, but I should tell you, she's a he."

"Are you *sure*?" Ellie asked, running her hand down Sam's back. "I thought all calicoes were girls."

"*Almost* all calicoes," said Clarence.

"What's a calico?" I asked, wondering if *calico* had something to do with the cat's notched ears. He looked as if he'd been in a couple of good fights—on the losing side.

"A black and white and orange cat," said Ellie. "They're always girls—at least that's what I heard."

"He looks like he's wearing an eye patch," I said. "Like a pirate."

"Why's he called Lantern Sam?" Ellie asked.

"That's a long story, maybe for another time. What I can tell you is that Sam is one in a million," Clarence announced proudly.

"Oh, brother. Here we go again," said a voice from behind the curtain of the next bed over—or at least that's where I *thought* it came from. *"It's not 'one in a million,' Clarence. Remember what that odd duck from Soseau University—the one with the bow tie and the elbow patches—told you? Professor Dinkelakker?*

16

Dunglepfeffer? Dimpledoofus? Well, whoever he was, he said I was one in three thousand. That I was a curiosity, nothing more. As if a man who goes out in public in a polka-dotted bow tie has room to talk. If anybody's a curiosity, it's him."

"One in three thousand is still pretty rare," I said with a shrug.

Clarence stiffened and looked at me so suspiciously that I wondered what I had done wrong. "What did you say . . . about Sam being one in three thousand?"

I was *very* confused. Maybe Clarence is a little hard of hearing, I thought, and didn't hear his neighbor. "I, um, just heard what that other man said."

"What other man?" Ellie asked. "I didn't hear anything."

"Just now," I said. "Somebody, right behind one of those curtains. Oh, come on. You *must* have heard him. He said something about a professor telling Clarence that Lantern Sam wasn't one in a million, that it was only one in three thousand."

Ellie looked at me as if I had just told her that the Shore-liner was made of moldy cheese. "I didn't hear anybody." She looked at Clarence. "Did you?"

"Uh-oh," said the voice. *"Looks like the little beggar can hear me."*

"There it is again!" I said. "He said, 'Uh-oh. Looks like the little beggar can hear me.' Hey! I'm not a beggar!"

"I still didn't hear anything," said Ellie. "*Who* called you a beggar?"

Lantern Sam sat up on the bed and stared directly into my eyes for an uncomfortably long time. "Wh-what's he doing?" I asked, too frightened to move. "It looks like he's trying to hypnotize me."

"You might as well tell him," said the voice. *"He'll figure it out eventually, even if he is just a dumb kid."*

"Figure *what* out?" I asked. Most of all, I wanted to know who was insulting me.

"You're right," said Clarence. "Here, you'd better sit down, kids."

Ellie and I, both bewildered, sat on the edge of the bed, one on each side of Lantern Sam.

"That voice you heard, Henry—it's, um, well, I know it seems hard to believe, but it's Sam," Clarence said matter-of-factly. "That's right. Lantern Sam . . . talks. Wait, let me rephrase that. He doesn't *talk* like you and I do, but I can hear what he's thinking. And now it, uh, well, looks like you're in the same boat."

I may not have been the next Einstein, but I knew when somebody was pulling my leg, so I laughed out loud. "Sure, mister. A talking cat. That's a doozy!" I looked Lantern Sam straight in the eyes. "Say something, Sam."

Serves me right for being a smart aleck, because I almost

fell off the bed when I heard Sam's voice, inside my head: *"What would you like to hear? How about a little Shakespeare? 'Friends, Romans, countrymen, lend me your ears; I come to bury Caesar, not to praise him. The evil that men do lives after them; the good is oft interred with their bones; so let it be with Caesar.' A little hammy, I know, but that's what you get when you learn Shakespeare aboard a train. Perhaps you prefer poetry. I've always been partial to Byron: 'She walks in beauty like the night—'"*

I recovered from the initial shock and my eyes went from Sam to Clarence, back to Sam, and then back and forth several more times as the performance went on. "Ohhhh, I get it! You're a ventriloquist! And your cat is the dummy." I had seen one of those acts at the county fair in Jefferson the summer before.

"Hey! Who are you calling a dummy?" Sam asked.

"Oh, sorry," I said automatically. Even though I didn't believe in talking cats, there was no need to forget my manners. "But wait. If he's the dummy, shouldn't his lips be moving?"

Ellie leaped to her feet. "What is going on? Why are you apologizing? Why did you say that Clarence is a ventriloquist?"

"You swear to me that you didn't hear him?" I demanded. "He was talking about Shakespeare. And poetry."

"What? I swear I didn't hear anything about Shakespeare

19

or poetry. In fact, I didn't hear anything at all. I'm starting to think you're both crazy."

I closed my eyes, trying as hard as I could to come up with a reasonable explanation for what was happening.

"It's just not possible," I said. "Cats can't talk. They're not even that smart. Everybody knows that dogs—"

"Don't!" shouted Clarence. "Stop! Don't say what you're thinking."

"What, that dogs are smarter than cats? It's true, isn't it?"

"Noooo," Clarence moaned. "Never, ever say that to Sam. I said something like that to him right after I found him and he lectured me for an hour about the achievements of *Felis domesticus* all through the ages."

"Wait—are you starting to *believe* this?" an astounded Ellie asked me.

"Um, yeah. Kind of. It doesn't make sense, I know, but *somebody's* talking inside my head."

"Well, I'm going to need more proof. You're both saying that you can hear what this cat is saying, right? Henry, you go through those doors at the end of the car and count to ten before coming back."

I did as she said.

Ellie was standing there with her arms crossed when I returned, confident that she was about to prove I was somehow involved in trying to trick her into believing that a cat could talk.

"Okay, Sam," she said. "Tell him. When is Clarence's birthday?"

"December twenty-fifth," said Sam.

"December twenty-fifth?" I answered.

"Ha! I knew it! I *knew* you were faking! When did you two plan this? Are you related or something?"

"What? That's not right?" If possible, I was even more confused. I looked to Clarence for help.

Clarence, shaking his head, picked up Sam. "Sam, tell him the real answer."

My head was filled with the strange sound of a cat sighing loudly. *"Humans. Absolutely no sense of humor. All right, all right. The real answer is February twenty-second, 1886."*

"February twenty-second, 1886?" I repeated.

"Wh-what?" cried Ellie. "How did you—"

"Is that right?"

Clarence nodded. "Sam was just having a little fun with you."

"It's really true," said Ellie. "You can talk to a *cat*. Is there . . . can anybody else?"

"Not that I know of," said Clarence.

"How does it work?" I asked. "I mean, why me? And why not her?"

"Don't know. Neither does Sam. My own theory is that it's kind of like the radio. Me and Sam, and now you, are all tuned to the same station, in a sense." Clarence glanced at his watch and quickly tucked it back into his vest pocket. "Sorry, kids, but I have to get back to work, and I'm afraid we're interrupting Sam's afternoon 'serious-thinking' time. Maybe tonight, after things quiet down—after dinner, and past the Syracuse stop—the four of us can chat some more."

"Aren't you forgetting something, Clarence?" Sam asked, lifting his head from the bed with one eye open. *"You know. The oath."*

"Oh, right," said Clarence. "Sam wants me to remind you that what you learned here today, about his, er, abilities . . . it has to stay secret. You can't tell a living soul. Not your parents, not your best friends. Heaven knows what would happen to Sam if somebody from the government learned the truth. He'd be on a ship to Europe to spy on the bad guys before you could say 'Babe Ruth.' There'd be experiments and who knows what else, especially when they discover that he's probably the greatest detective since Sherlock Holmes."

"He's a *detective*?" Ellie asked. "I'm going to be a detective, too!"

"Who do you think solved the Case of the Poughkeepsie Pickpocket?" asked Clarence, obviously proud of his feline companion. "And the Buffalo Bootleggers? Lantern Sam, that's who. I'll tell you all about that later. He has a good life here on the Shoreliner; he spends about eighteen hours a day *thinking*, solving the problems of the world. Promise to keep his secret?" He held up his hand as if he were in a courtroom, being sworn in.

"Promise," Ellie and I said, solemnly raising our hands.

"Thanks, kids. And now, Sam, you can go back to your important work," Clarence said with a wink at us.

"*Mrrraaa,*" said Sam, who then closed his eyes and resumed his "serious thinking."

Don't Call Me Samantha
THE ALMOST ENTIRELY TRUE
AUTOBIOGRAPHY OF LANTERN SAM

Flatter but Wiser

It's not that I don't trust Henry to tell you the truth, but let's face facts: He came late to the dance, as they say. He was only around for a small part of the story—for one, maybe two, of my lives. And we all know that humans have terrible memories, and that cats have nine lives, right? So I'm here to tell you the *rest* of the story—the interesting parts. Believe me, there's a lot of story left to tell, and I can't think of a better cat to tell it.

For starters, my name wasn't always Lantern Sam. I was born in a dairy barn outside of Linesville, Pennsylvania, on November 1, 1929, three days after the stock market crashed on Wall Street. Not that I, or any of the people around me, noticed. Daniel and Delilah Dilly were simple farmers who kept a herd of twenty-five Jersey cows. It is doubtful that they even knew where Wall Street was, and they certainly didn't own any stocks or bonds. Mom was a calico like me and had lived on the Dilly farm her entire life. My father, who came from a farm up the road, was all black, which made him unpopular with the superstitious Dillys. There were seven of us in the litter: five calicoes and two brothers who were the spitting image of dear old Dad, who went by the name of Ajax. The Dillys gave their youngest daughter, Debbie, the job of naming us. Naturally, she assumed that all the calicoes were females (which, as you know, is wrong), so she named us Sally, Selma, Sarah, Susie, and Samantha. You can probably guess which one was me. My two brothers were named Simon and Sylvester.

Other than being stuck with a girl's name, though, I can't really complain about my kittenhood. I had a loving mother, six siblings to play king of the hayloft with, and best of all, we had all the fresh Jersey milk we could drink. And when I say fresh, I mean straight from the udder to my tongue in under a minute. It was warm, and rich, and sweet as sugar, and I've spent the rest of my lives looking for milk half as good. Sometimes life is like that, I guess. You don't realize how great you have it until it's gone, and you're stuck on a twenty-hour train ride with nothing to drink but ice-cold Holstein milk that's had the cream removed.

Right about now, you're probably asking yourself, if it was so great at the Dillys' farm, why did Lantern Sam ever leave?

A good question. A great question, even.

It may not be the answer you're looking for, but here it is: I don't know. Not really, anyway. I suppose I felt what lots of young cats (and young people, too) feel at some point in their lives—that they have to see the world for themselves. I needed some adventure, some danger. I had read the books and heard the stories about faraway places like Meadville and Grove City, and I wanted to see them for myself.

But I'm getting ahead of myself. I was telling you about my kittenhood, and my first brush with "the nine lives question."

It was mid-January, and I was about ten weeks old and maybe two or three pounds. The temperature outside the barn had dropped to fifteen below zero, so cold that all those warm cow bodies raised the inside temperature to only slightly above zero. My siblings and I had burrowed into a crevice between bales of straw in the hayloft, but I was still shivering.

"You know where I bet it's really warm," I said to my brothers and sisters. "Snuggled into the straw right up against one of the cows, especially the big, old ones."

"Don't do it," said Susie. "It's too dangerous."

I puffed myself up as big as I could. "I don't care. I need a little danger. Besides, I'm going to freeze to death if I stay here, so what's the difference?"

"Suit yourself," she said. Years later, when Susie became a mother, she was *much* more protective of her kittens than she was of her siblings, as is often the case.

I jumped down into the hay in the manger between two of the biggest cows, Dell and Derby (all the Dilly cows had names that started with *D,* and the Dillys had long ago used up all the usual ones).

Derby turned her head to look at me. She was lying on a bed of fresh, deep straw, and I could feel the warmth radiating from her thousand-pound body.

"Mrrraaaa," I said, rubbing against her. I continued "testing the water" to see if she had a problem with my plan, but she went on chewing her cud, not at all concerned with me. So far, so good. I zeroed in on a spot near her belly, which seemed like the warmest place, and buried myself in the straw, pressing my tiny body against hers until I felt the heat start to flow. For about an hour, it was a little slice of heaven, if heaven is a warm place that smells like a barn (and I think it is).

And then.

And then, while I lay there in a state of perfect contentment,

Derby shifted positions. Before I knew what was happening, I was completely *under* her, trapped in the cranny between her udder, her back leg, and the straw-covered floor of the stall. As she settled into position, her tremendous mass began to squeeze the breath right out of me. I tried to wriggle in order to get her attention, hoping and praying that she wouldn't shift the *wrong* way and crush me completely, but it was no use. There was just too much Derby.

I don't know how long I lay there like that. Susie seemed to think it was at least a couple of hours, maybe a bit more. At four-fifteen, the Dillys entered the barn and flipped on the lights. Cows started to stir for the morning milking, and Derby pulled herself to her feet.

According to Susie, it was Debbie Dilly who spotted me first. She was certain I was dead.

"Oh no! Poor Samantha." She knelt in the straw next to my flattened body and gently lifted me in her hands.

"Dead?" her father asked.

Debbie nodded. "Flat as a pancake. She's still warm."

"That's because Derby was on top of her," said Mr. Dilly.

And then I sneezed, scaring poor Debbie so much that she dropped me! Luckily, I landed in a pile of straw, and not manure.

"Daddy!" she cried, recovering enough to pick me up again. "She's alive. She just sneezed."

"Mrrr," I said as the feeling started to return to my legs and paws.

"It's a miracle," announced Debbie.

"Let's not get carried away," said her father, a practical man. "It's just a cat. A darned lucky cat, if you ask me. I think it's safe to say that she just used up one of her lives."

Chapter 2

After we left the dormitory car, I figured that Ellie would go back to her suite and leave me alone, but she kept on following me, like a strip of flypaper stuck to my shoe. The nickel that my mother had given me was burning a hole in my pocket, and I headed for the club car in search of something to spend it on.

"Grape Nehi, please," I said, stepping up to the counter.

"And I'll have orange, please," said Ellie, producing a shiny nickel of her own.

We took seats across from each other and slowly sipped our sodas, relishing every drop. Ellie finished hers first, and sat quietly for a moment before blurting out, "I still don't believe it. Not really. First, everyone knows that all calicoes are girls, and second, everyone knows that cats can't talk. It's some kind of trick. It *has* to be."

"It's not a trick—scout's honor. It's hard to describe how his voice sounds in here," I said, pointing at my head. "Far away, and echoey, like he's in a cave, or at the end of a long tunnel. But it really is there, I swear."

Ellie stuck out her lower lip about three inches. "Har-rumph. It's not *fair*. Why does he talk to you and not me? You didn't even know what a calico was." She crossed her arms and stared out the window with a pouty face until a New York–bound train on the other track zoomed past, just inches away, making her jump.

"I don't know why you're mad at me," I said. "It's not like I asked for it or anything. And what good is it, anyway? Big deal, so I can hear a cat talking. Once I get off the train in Ashtabula, I'll probably never see Lantern Sam, or you, again."

"Don't say that!" Ellie said. "We're going to be friends forever."

"You're crazy," I said, making a face. "You don't know anything about me. I'll bet you don't even remember my name."

"Henry Shipley. H-E-N-R-Y S-H-I-P-L-E-Y. You live in Ashtabula, Ohio, and you have a little sister named Jessica.

Your father is captain of a ship called the *Point Pelee*. You like science and drawing boats, and you want to be a naval arch—"

"Okay, okay, I get it. I forgot that you remember everything. Still doesn't mean we're going to stay friends."

Ellie shrugged and smiled a know-it-all smile, her nose stuck high in the air. "Say what you want. I'm right. I can just tell. You'll see, 'specially after we catch those criminals. I wonder where they're hiding out, planning their next move."

"What do they look like, anyway?" I asked.

"Kind of ordinary—well, he is, anyway. She's quite pretty. I didn't get a good look at what they were wearing because they were behind the baggage cart."

"One is a woman! You didn't say that before."

"You didn't ask."

"What are they wanted for?"

"All the usual crimes, I suppose," Ellie answered. "Murder, probably. Robbing banks. That's what they're *all* wanted for—the really famous criminals. Like Bonnie and Clyde, and Ma Barker's gang."

I stood up suddenly, checking all around me. "Oh no! I must have left my sketchbook back in the observation car. I have to get it before anybody else finds it. Meet you back here in a minute?"

"You have *one* minute," Ellie answered. "Then I'm going to sneak back into that car up in the front to see Sam again. Maybe if I listen *really* hard, I can hear him. One . . . two . . . three . . ."

"You're counting? Criminy!"

"Four . . . five . . . six . . ."

I turned and ran through the car, almost knocking down a pregnant woman in a dress as red as her lipstick.

"Hey, watch it!" growled her husband. The brim of his hat cast a dark shadow over his face, but I did manage a quick look at his eyes as they sparked with fire at me.

"Sorry!" I shouted, turning and catching one last glimpse of Ellie. She was staring openmouthed at the pregnant woman and her husband, who was dressed all in black except for the white minister's collar at his throat.

By my count, I made it to the end of the observation car and picked up my sketchbook ("Whew! It's still here!") in a shade over thirty seconds. The collision had cost me some time, no doubt about that, but the round-trip *couldn't* have taken much more than a minute—which was why I was so surprised, on returning to the club car, to find no sign of Ellie.

"Where the heck did she go?" I asked no one in particular.

"She went thataway," said a man in a gray flannel suit, peering over his newspaper at me and pointing toward the front of the car with his chin. "You're looking for the pretty little brunette, aren't you? The one with the Shirley Temple curls, wearing a green dress? Is she your girlfriend?"

"N-no! She's not . . . she's only ten!" I headed for the front of the train, through the sleepers and the dining car, stopping at the section where my mother and sister sat.

Mother opened her eyes, smiling as if she were waking from a pleasant dream. "Well, there you are. I was beginning to wonder if you were still aboard, but then I remembered we hadn't stopped yet, and even *you* wouldn't jump out of a moving train—I think. What have you been doing?" She pointed at my sketchbook. "Let me see. Did you draw me a picture?"

"I didn't really . . . finish it. Um, did you see a . . . girl . . . go past, a few seconds ago? In a green dress?"

"A girl? No, I don't think so. No one has been past for a few minutes. I think I would have seen . . . who is she? Did you make a friend? Is she pretty?"

"Aw, Mother," I said, feeling myself blush. "She's only ten." What *is* it with grown-ups? Can't a fella have a friend who happens to be a girl?

"Sorry, I'll mind my own business. What should I do if I see her? How will I even know it's her?"

"Just forget it. I'll find her myself."

I walked into the dormitory car, slowing and listening carefully as I approached Clarence's bed, where the curtain was half open.

"Hello? Ellie? Mr., um, Clarence?" No one answered, so I pulled the curtain open the rest of the way. Sam lifted his head, opening his eyes just enough to squint at me.

"Mrrraaa. You again? Did you bring me anything to eat?"

His voice startled me; I still wasn't quite used to the idea of a talking cat, and to tell the honest-to-God truth, I felt incredibly silly at the thought of trying to talk back to him.

"Oh. Hi, kitty, er, Sam," I said after making sure no one else was around. "Sorry to wake you."

"I wasn't sleeping," Sam huffed. *"I was thinking."*

"Oh, uh, right. I'm looking for Ellie, the girl I was here with earlier. She said she was coming to see you again. I think she's mad that I can hear you and she can't. Have you seen her?"

"I don't blame you for looking for that one—she's the cat's meow. Looks like she's rolling in dough, too. Is she your girlfriend?"

"No!" I said, louder than I had intended. "Why does everyone keep asking me that? She's *not* my girlfriend. Criminy, I just met her."

"Okay, okay. Calm down, kid. I'm just having a little fun with

you. You humans are so sensitive. Now, are you sure you don't have anything to eat?"

"What? Uh, no, nothing . . . just this one stick of hard candy I had in my pocket."

"No candy. That stuff will kill you. Listen, because this is important: *I'm very keen on California sardines, especially the Sail On brand. They use just the right amount of salt. Mmwwaa. My mouth is watering thinking about them. You're sure you don't have any stashed away?"*

"Sardines? Why would I be carrying around a can of sardines? Yuck!"

"Don't knock 'em till you've tried 'em, kid."

"Oh, I've tried them plenty of times. But what about Ellie? Have you seen her? Or heard her?"

"Negative," said Sam. *"Not since you two left here."*

I retraced my route through the train in my mind. After leaving Ellie in the club car, I went to the last car in the train and then all the way to the first car. Eleven cars. The only place I hadn't looked was the locomotive, but I was pretty sure she wasn't up there. Where was she?

"Maybe she went into her compartment," said Sam. *"Do you know where her family is?"*

"They're in that big, fancy room all the way back in the observation car."

"No kidding?" said Sam, clearly impressed. "The Commodore Perry suite? Who is this kid?"

"Ellie . . . Strasbourg. Her father is somebody important, I guess."

"I'd say so," said Sam. "Do you have any idea how much that suite costs?"

"No, not really. But she couldn't have gone in there anyway. She would have had to get past me, because I was just *in* the observation car."

"Don't know what to tell you, kid. If I had to guess, I'd say that, uh, nature called, if you know what I mean. She was probably in the litter box, er, the lav, when you passed her. It's like what Clarence tells parents when they think their kids have disappeared: when all else fails, check the lavatories. Give her a couple of minutes. Bet she'll show up right here."

But she didn't. Not after five minutes. Or after ten. When the train pulled into Albany, I heard the porters rummaging about in the baggage compartment in the front half of the dormitory car, moving trunks and suitcases around as a few passengers disembarked and a few more climbed aboard.

"Well, I guess she isn't coming," I said.

"Sorry, kid," said Sam. "Dames are like that sometimes. Just when you think you have them figured out . . . whammo! They sock *you one right on the kisser. Or eat your sardines. Or worse, you find out there's another tomcat in the picture. I can't tell you how many times that's happened to moi. Now, if you were to, say, pass by the kitchen, and somebody just happened to leave a quart of cream out, or a can of sardines, or even anchovies, you would help out an old buddy, wouldn't you?"*

And then—I swear—he waggled his cat eyebrows at me.

"Uh, sure, Sam," I said.

As I left the dormitory car, I found the corridor blocked by a slow-moving family that had just boarded the train. A man in a straw fedora carried his sleeping daughter, whose face was buried in his shoulder; her long red hair hung down his back. His wife, a tall, stylish woman in high heels and a black-and-white-striped dress, followed closely behind. Her hair, like the daughter's, was long and wavy and the color of a new penny.

A few feet before they reached the section where my mother and sister sat peacefully watching the scenery fly past, something fell—from the girl's hair, I thought—hit the floor, and bounced under a seat.

"Excuse me! You dropped something," I said, but neither parent seemed to hear me. I knelt down and reached my arm as far beneath the seat as I could, moving it from side to side until my fingers landed on something smooth. It was a silver barrette—a far cry from the plain ones that the girls in my school wore—with a large oval in the center, engraved with a swirling, delicate pattern.

I ran after the family and tapped the woman on the shoulder. "Excuse me."

Startled, she spun around so quickly that her long hair flew into her face. "What?" she said, her narrowed eyes burning into mine.

"You dropped this," I said, holding out the barrette. "Back there."

She stared at it for a few seconds before saying, "I'm afraid you're mistaken. It's not mine—or, um, *hers*." She turned away without another word and hurried to catch up to her husband. I absentmindedly put the barrette in my pocket and sighed.

A moment later, the train pulled away from the station in Albany and began the trek west toward Schenectady, Syracuse, and points beyond.

Half an hour later, I was well on my way to forgetting about Ellie, who had obviously ditched me. What difference did it make? I asked myself. She was just a spoiled, bratty girl, and besides, she was only *ten*. I had much better things to do than hang out with her.

While the Shoreliner chased the sun across upstate New York, I sat across from Mother and Jessica with my sketchpad on my lap, filling in some details on my tugboat drawing. I lifted my pencil as the train clattered over a bridge and looked up to find Clarence the Conductor at my side. Next to him was a tall, thin woman wearing an elegant charcoal-gray suit and a string of pearls that were the size of my prized "elephant egg" marbles. She was fidgeting—nervously rubbing her hands together, darting her eyes here and there about the car—so much that she made me nervous.

"Here he is, ma'am," said Clarence. "This is the young man who was with your daughter."

"Have you seen her? Have you seen my Ellie?" the woman asked, her voice trembling.

I sat up straight in my seat and closed my sketchpad. "No, ma'am. Not for a while, that is. I was with her in the club car a while ago. I went to the observation car to get *this,* and when I came back she was gone."

My mother, who had been napping with Jessica and *Gone with the Wind* on her lap, opened her eyes. Blinded momentarily by the sun, she reached over and pulled down the window shade. "What's going on?"

"I'm Doris Strasbourg," said the woman. "My little girl, my Ellie—I can't find her."

"Your son was with her earlier," Clarence explained. "We were hoping he knew where she might have gone."

"We were going back to the dormitory car to see Lantern Sam. I went up there, but he told me—" I stopped, realizing that what I was about to say sounded loony enough to land me in a straightjacket and a room at the Hotel Silly.

"Who is . . . Lantern Sam?" Mother asked. "Is he one of the porters?"

"Sam is my cat," said Clarence. "The kids met him a little earlier in the afternoon. He rides with me up in the dormitory car."

"Like I was saying," I continued, "I went up there, but Ellie wasn't around. I waited for a while, but she never showed up. I just thought . . ."

"Yes?" Ellie's mother leaned closer, waiting for me to finish my thought.

"Just that, well, maybe she didn't want to hang out with me anymore. I figured she went back to her compartment."

Clarence started to gently guide Mrs. Strasbourg toward the rear of the train. "Let's get you back to your suite, ma'am. I have all the porters looking for her. She'll turn up. There're lots of hiding places aboard the old Shoreliner. Henry, you'll let us know if you see her? The Strasbourgs are in the Commodore Perry suite, all the way back in the observation car—you remember, right?"

"Yes, sir."

41

"I'm sure she's fine," said my mother. "Henry is always disappearing on me and then magically reappearing at the moment I'm beginning to panic. He'll be the death of me one day. Children! It's as if their only job is to make their parents worry."

Don't Call Me Samantha

THE ALMOST ENTIRELY TRUE
AUTOBIOGRAPHY OF LANTERN SAM

He Shot an Arrow into the Air. . . .

I survived the incident with Derby the cow with two side effects. First, I was longer and thinner than I had been, a change that has stayed with me. From the side, I look perfectly normal, but if you were to see me from the front, you'd be surprised at how narrow I am, a bit like a piecrust that's been rolled out. If anything, that has worked to my advantage, as you'll see. I can slip under doors, through windows opened "just a crack," or into about anyplace else that foolish people *think* they can keep me out of. Second, and this is the strange one, I lost the ability to purr. Ever since the night I spent under Derby, I just can't do it anymore. People think I don't purr because I'm unhappy, but that's not it. I'm plenty happy, as cats go. My purrer just got switched off, or squashed, or something. Period. I don't especially care to discuss it any further.

A few weeks after the Derby incident, I dodged another bullet, or in this case, an arrow. Although, to be honest, I didn't quite dodge it, as you'll see. That experience left me with my first scar. It also explains my basic distrust of all boys under the age of thirty (at least).

The two middle Dilly sons, Danny and Davey, had received most unwise Christmas presents from their well-meaning parents: archery sets with wooden bows, several metal-tipped arrows, and a dozen paper targets. The boys set up a bale of straw at one end of the barn (far away from the cows), hung a target from it, and proceeded to spray arrows in all directions. It was only rarely that they hit the bale of straw, let alone the target, but my siblings and I all knew to stay out of that area when they were shooting, because . . . well, because they were boys.

One day, Simon, Sylvester, and I were on the prowl, looking for a mouse to chase, when one ran practically between my legs.

"Mrrr!" I shouted, and took off after him.

Rule Number One when hunting mice, Mom told us time and time again, is simple: don't forget all the *other* rules of cat life. You know, rules like don't play in the street, and don't sleep on warm car engines (Simon learned that one the hard way—his nickname became Stubby), or, in this particular case, stay away from two boys armed with bows and arrows.

As I ran across the barn after the mouse, I completely forgot Rule Number One, and I found myself on a path that would take me between the boys and their target.

"Look out!" shouted Sylvester, covering his eyes.

Danny and Davey, to their credit, tried to hold their fire, but by the time they saw me it was too late. The first arrow struck the concrete a foot in front of me, throwing up a shower of sparks before skidding harmlessly into the straw bale.

The sight of that arrow hitting the ground just inches away scared me so much that I bounded straight up in the air—like I was on a pogo stick, according to Simon, who watched the whole thing. My jump, unfortunately, was perfectly timed, and the second arrow intercepted me midflight, neatly piercing the skin at the back of my neck and pinning me to the paper target. A perfect bull's-eye.

For a few seconds, as I hung from the arrow, there was complete silence in the barn. Danny and Davey stood frozen in place, too frightened to move, or even to speak. As for me, I tried to convince myself that I really wasn't dead. It wasn't until the holes in my neck started to hurt that I believed it.

"Is it dead?" Davey asked. "I didn't mean to do it!"

"Debbie is going to kill you," said Danny. "Swell shot, though. Bull's-eye."

"Shut up. We've got to get rid of the cat. And you have to promise you'll never tell."

"Okay, but you owe me."

They crept toward the target, where I dangled most uncomfortably from their arrow, a feline shish kebab.

"Mrrrrraaaaa," I said.

"It's alive!" cried Davey. "Look, it's just through the skin."

"What should we do?" Danny asked.

"Get me down, you simpletons!" I thought.

Lucky for me, the door at the side of the barn opened and Debbie stepped inside. She saw me and screamed.

"Samantha! You poor baby! What did you two do to her?" She put her hands under me, taking the weight off the skin of my neck, and I felt a hundred times better almost immediately.

"It was an accident! I swear!" said Davey, who started crying.

"Well, let's get her down first, then we'll worry about that. I'll hold Samantha, and Danny, you pull the arrow."

"Wh-what? Whoa, Nelly!" I thought. "Isn't this a job for a professional? Shouldn't we wait for a veterinarian? Or Mr. Dilly, at least?"

Danny nodded at her as I squirmed.

"Go!" she said.

Danny pulled quickly, and in one exquisitely painful movement, the arrow and I were separated.

"Mrrrrrroooooowwwwww," I moaned in Debbie's arms.

"That's two, Samantha," she said with a sad shake of her head.

Chapter 3

By the time the Shoreliner zoomed past Schenectady, twenty-five minutes later, all of Clarence's known "hiding places" had been checked, and there was still no sign of Ellie. I was with Clarence and Sam in the dormitory car when one of the porters, a tall, handsome young man of eighteen or nineteen, returned from the baggage compartment.

"What is it, James?" Clarence asked.

"You'd better see this, Mr. Nockwood, sir," he said. "I was checking everyplace, like you said, and, well, see for yourself."

Sam and I followed them through the mail room and into the baggage compartment, separated by a heavy cloth divider that functioned as a door and that closed by means of metal snaps.

"Right over here, sir," said James, leading Clarence to the far corner of the car. Behind a number of trunks and suitcases were dozens of marble floor tiles—six- and twelve-inch samples in every color imaginable—dumped into a pile.

"Looks like somebody overturned a salesman's trunk," Clarence observed. "But where's the trunk?"

"That's just it, sir. There's no empty cases in here. I checked the whole car—twice. I was just thinking—"

As Clarence held up his hand to interrupt James, a million crazy ideas raced through my brain. Was it possible? Had Ellie been kidnapped—knocked out and stuffed into a traveling salesman's trunk, and then taken off the train?

"Now let's not jump to any conclusions and start scaring that poor woman—and the rest of the passengers—to death," said Clarence. "James, I want you to do me a favor. There must be fifty or sixty pounds of marble tiles here. I want to know who they belong to. Donnie was loading baggage in New York; he must have helped a traveling salesman put a heavy trunk aboard. Find him and bring him here."

"Yes, sir," said James, hurrying out of the car.

Sam hopped up on one of the trunks that had been moved to hide the mess, then leaped down onto the pile of tiles. He sniffed around them for a while before jumping back up onto a trunk.

"Something's not right," he said. *"If you're going to hide them, why not do a better job of it? It's almost like they wanted us to find them, and quickly."*

I noticed a balled-up white handkerchief on the floor and bent down to pick it up. When I brought it close to my face for a better look, the smell of it almost knocked me off my feet. Fighting off dizziness, I dropped the handkerchief and waved my hands around, trying to clear the air.

"Whoa! What is that smell?" I asked, breathing rapidly through my mouth.

Sam lifted his nose into the air and sniffed. *"I'm not positive, but if I had to guess, it would be chloroform. That's what you use when you want to knock somebody out in a hurry. Are you all right? You look a little light-headed."*

Clarence picked up the handkerchief, wrapped it up in his own, and shoved it into his coat pocket. "I don't like the looks of this—not one bit," he said as James returned to the baggage area.

"I found him," said James, coming back with a young man whose muscles bulged through his porter's uniform.

Donnie scratched the back of his neck for a few seconds

when Clarence asked him about the trunk. Suddenly his eyes lighted up. "Oh, right! I remember him. Big fella. Red face. Asked me if I was interested in a new marble floor for me house. I told him I didn't have a house, sir, but that didn't slow him down one bit."

"Do you remember his name, or what car he was in?" Clarence asked.

"Never got his name, but he was in compartment D in the second sleeper car back, I think. Don't know why he didn't just buy a coach ticket—since he was only going s'far as Albany."

"Thank you, Donnie. You've been very helpful. You too, James. One more question, then you can return to your duties: did any other passengers with large cases get *off* the train at the Albany station?"

Donnie shook his head. "No, sir. Just small suitcases."

"That's right, Mr. Nockwood. I was on the platform, too. I would have seen," said James.

"I see," said Clarence. "You're sure?"

Both men nodded at Clarence and then left the car.

"We need to see his compartment right away," said Sam, jumping off his trunk.

Clarence hesitated when he realized that I was still tagging along. "Uh, Henry, I think you'd better let us take it from here," he said.

51

I dropped my shoulders and stared at my shoes, putting on the most dejected and disappointed face I could muster. It worked like a charm.

"Oh, let the kid come along," said Sam. *"He's already involved, and he knows the girl better than we do. That could come in handy."*

"Okay, but I go into the compartment first," said Clarence, leading the way with his passkey in hand.

I smiled at my mother as we walked past, pausing just long enough to say, "I'm helping the conductor look for Ellie. I'll be back in a while."

Clarence stopped outside the door to compartment D and pressed his ear against it. "It's quiet."

He knocked twice, and when there was no response, he turned the key in the lock and pushed open the door. Sam slipped silently past his feet, and I followed, holding my breath and feeling my heart pound.

The smell of stale cigar smoke filled the cramped room, and Clarence pointed at the ashtray, where two thin cigars and a single hand-rolled cigarette had been snubbed out.

Taped to the window were a story and photograph neatly clipped from a newspaper. "Holy cow! Look at that!" I said, pointing at it. "That's Ellie, with her parents."

From deep within a vest pocket, Clarence dug out his reading glasses and put them on. "Pittsburgh newspaper from last summer. The family was at an amusement park for some kind of groundbreaking, it looks like."

"The Blue Streak!" I cried. "That's where she said she was going."

Sam's silence and Clarence's blank look told me that they had no idea what the Blue Streak was, hard as that was for me to believe.

"The Blue Streak is a roller coaster," I explained. "But not just any roller coaster—it's the fastest one ever, and it opens tomorrow! Ellie told me that she was on her way to Conneaut Lake Park. Her father is a friend of the man who designed it. She gets to be one of the first people to ride it."

"Our kidnapper has been planning this for a long time," said Sam. *"He knew she'd be on this train, and he knew exactly where she was going."*

"Why would he just leave all this here?" Clarence wondered aloud. "First the tile samples, which he must have known would lead us right here. The handkerchief. This article. Never heard of a kidnapper—or any kind of crook, for that matter—being so sloppy, leaving so many clues behind."

"He doesn't care if we find it. In fact, he wanted us to find it, all of it," said Sam. *"But something still doesn't add up. I never heard of a kidnapping without a—"*

"Ransom note?" I said, kneeling down to unstick an envelope that had gotten jammed beneath the compartment door. Printed in primary school lettering across the front was the name Doris Strasbourg. "Betcha this is it. It must have gotten caught when we opened the door."

"Let's see it," said Sam. "Open it very carefully."

My hands were shaking as I followed Sam's directions and removed a single sheet of paper that had been folded in half. Large, all-capital letters spelled out the kidnapper's demands:

IF YOU WANT ELLIE BACK ALIVE, PUT THE BLUE STREAK IN A MAILBAG AND MAKE THE DROP AT THE DUNKIRK STATION. WHEN MY ASSOCIATES CONFIRM PICKUP, ELLIE WILL BE RETURNED SAFELY TO CONNEAUT LAKE PARK AT NOON TOMORROW. THERE WILL BE NO FURTHER INSTRUCTIONS.

"That doesn't make sense," I said. "How can you put the Blue Streak into a mailbag?"

"There's a lot about this case that doesn't make sense," remarked Sam.

"We need to get this to Mrs. Strasbourg right away," said Clarence, motioning to Sam and me to exit the compartment. "I guess it's up to me to tell her that her daughter's been kidnapped, and she has a little over five hours to pay a ransom I don't understand. I'm not looking forward to that, not one bit. Poor woman. She's going to be hysterical, and I can't blame her. Ever since that Lindbergh case, folks are . . ." He closed the door, making certain that it was locked, and then shook his head. "That poor kid. She must be terrified. Henry, would you mind carrying Sam? Thank you. I want him to hear everything, but some passengers are afraid of cats, and if they see one wandering around, there's no telling what they'll do. He's caused a panic on more than one occasion."

"Are people really afraid of cats?" I asked.

"There's a lot of old wives' tales out there," said Clarence. "My own granny, rest her soul, wouldn't have one in the house if there was a baby. Said that cats would sneak into the baby's crib and steal its breath—whatever *that* means."

"If you ask me, people aren't nearly scared enough," said Sam. *"If they knew what I know about cats, they'd really be afraid."*

"Is he serious?" I whispered to Clarence.

"Don't pay any attention to him," said Clarence. "He's full of hot air. He's just mad because the cooks brought aboard the wrong kind of cream. Apparently, it's from Holstein cows, and Mr. Persnickety here prefers Jersey cows. Don't ask me how he can tell the difference."

"Even a stupid dog could tell the difference," said Sam, almost spitting out the words. *"Seriously, if you humans had any less sense of taste or smell, you'd be rocks."*

As we entered the dining car, Clarence stopped James, the young porter who had discovered the spilled marble tiles.

"James, I want you to do me a favor. Remember that compartment we discussed? Keep a close eye on it. No one goes in there without my permission. Not even to clean up. Got it?"

"Yes, sir, Mr. Nockwood," said James. "You can count on me."

The observation car was quiet, as most passengers had returned to their rooms to dress for dinner or were enjoying cocktails in the club car. Clarence's knuckles had barely touched the door to the Commodore Perry suite when Ellie's mom, Doris Strasbourg, flung it open. The hopeful look on her face was instantly dashed when she saw no sign of Ellie—only the long faces of Clarence and me, holding Sam, who wouldn't stop wriggling, digging his claws deeper into my arms.

"Where's Ellie? What's happened to her?"

"Maybe it's best if we talk inside, ma'am," said Clarence.

When I got my first look at the Commodore Perry suite, my mouth was hanging open so wide that a fly actually buzzed right into it. For a second I thought I had swallowed him, but somehow he found his way out.

"Stop fidgeting," said Sam.

"I can't help it," I said. "There was a—"

Sam laughed when he saw the look on my face as I realized that everyone was staring at me. *"Go on, finish your story,"* he said with a chuckle.

I apologized and then quickly wiped my tongue on my sleeve before taking in the mind-boggling sights of the Commodore Perry suite. All around me were dark, lovingly polished wood, gleaming brass hardware, and plush green velvet; it was a room fit for kings and queens, and princes and princesses. I thought for a moment of my mother and baby sister in their ordinary, uncomfortable section seats near the front of the train, and suddenly it struck me: Ellie Strasbourg *was* a princess. If the rest of her world was anything like this, she and I might as well have been from different planets.

"Not bad, eh, kid?" said Sam. *"I could get used to living in a joint like this. In fact, I should be living in a place like this, right, Clarence? Don't ignore me, old timer—I know you can hear me just fine."*

A giant of a man, six and a half feet tall with a waist that must have measured in yards instead of inches, stood in the center of the room; everyone else seemed to revolve around him, like moons around a planet. His head was completely bald except for an impressive handlebar mustache, its ends waxed into perfect curls.

"Judge J. P. Ambrose," he announced in a booming voice as he produced a shiny silver badge. "Crawford County sheriff. Retired, that is."

If he wasn't scary enough, seated in a wing chair and smoking a hand-rolled cigarette was the serious young man with the fiery eyes who had barked at me for nearly knocking over his pregnant wife. I quickly covered half of my face with one hand, hoping he wouldn't recognize me.

"I'm Reverend Travis Perfiddle," he said seriously. "My wife and I were in the observation car when we heard about Mrs. Strasbourg's misfor—er, her current situation. I'm here to provide moral support in this *most* difficult time. My dear wife is expecting a child very soon, or she would be here as well. She is in her bed, praying for the safe return of poor Ellie."

Across the room, the Strasbourgs' maid, a striking young woman in a starched blue uniform, looked warily at Sam, who was still in my arms. She backed away, never taking her eyes off him, and stopped only when she ran into a wall.

"Oh, I'm sorry, gentlemen," said Mrs. Strasbourg. "This is Julia, our maid. I'd forgotten—she's afraid of cats. We have dogs at the house, but no cats."

"No need to worry about Sam," said Clarence. "He wouldn't hurt a fly."

"Unlike Henry," said Sam, in my head. *"Apparently, he eats flies."*

Clarence shook Reverend Perfiddle's hand and then told them everything: the discovery of the marble samples, the handkerchief, the picture of Ellie, and finally, the ransom note.

Once Mrs. Strasbourg started sobbing, there was no stopping her. "My baby, my poor baby. Who would do something like this? Where is she? Why? Why!"

Julia glided across the room, her floor-length dress rustling quietly. She knelt close to her employer, speaking soothing words and wiping tears from the distraught woman's face.

Judge Ambrose stomped his foot, shaking the whole compartment. "Anarchists, that's who. They're everywhere. First they kidnap that poor little Lindbergh baby. Then along come Sacco and Vanzetti with their robbing, murdering ways. Where does it end?"

"Who?" I whispered to Sam.

"Shhh! I'll tell you later. I don't want to miss anything."

Clarence ignored the judge and handed the ransom note to Mrs. Strasbourg. "Do you know what this means? Henry tells me that the Blue Streak is an amusement park ride—a roller coaster that you are on your way to see. Why would the kidnapper—"

Mrs. Strasbourg turned to the maid. "Julia, would you please show them . . . ?"

Julia hurriedly crossed the room again, then knelt before a leather-covered trunk and opened its lid. An elaborately carved jewelry box sat inside, and from this she removed a sky-blue leather pouch. She carried it back to Mrs. Strasbourg.

Mrs. Strasbourg untied the drawstring and turned the bag over, spilling a necklace into her hand. She eyed it sadly for a few seconds and then set it on the table in front of everyone.

"It was a gift from my father," she said, "on my eighteenth birthday. It's called the Blue Streak."

Dozens of brilliant gems made up the length of the necklace, starting with tiny stones at the clasp and ending with one enormous blue-as-the-sea sapphire set in the center.

Reverend Perfiddle inhaled deeply from his cigarette and leaned forward, choking on his own smoke and almost falling out of his chair when he saw that sapphire, and Judge Ambrose's eyes looked as if they might pop right out of his shiny bald head.

"Sweet Caesar's ghost," he whispered.

"The center stone is over seventy-five carats," said Mrs. Strasbourg. "It's called the Blue Streak because if you examine it very closely with a magnifying glass, you'll see a single flaw deep inside the stone. When my father first saw it, he said that it reminded him of a comet streaking across the sky."

"Probably would have been cheaper to buy a real comet," noted Sam, though only Clarence and I heard.

Judge Ambrose cleared his throat loudly and addressed Clarence directly. "Is there a cinder dick aboard the train?"

"No, not this trip," answered Clarence.

"What's that?" I whispered to Sam.

"A railroad detective," he answered.

"Any other lawmen?" Ambrose asked. "Police? FBI, maybe?"

"None that I know of."

"And how long till we get to Dunkirk?" He tugged on his watch chain until a shiny gold pocket watch dropped into his hand.

"Five hours. A bit more."

Ambrose made a big show of winding his watch and then puffed himself up even bigger.

Sam clenched my arms with his claws. *"Back up, kid! You remember the Hindenburg? If that belly of his explodes, nobody is going to get out of here alive. Oh, the humanity!"*

The judge took the ransom note from Clarence and patted him on the back in a way that seemed to annoy the kindly conductor. "I think it's best if I take over from here.

I have experience dealing with situations like this, and besides, I'm sure you have other responsibilities. I'll be in touch if I need to see inside the compartment where you found the note. I'll be needing to send a telegram—have to let someone in Dunkirk know what's going on, and to have them alert the local authorities." And with that, he pushed Clarence and me (along with a loudly complaining Lantern Sam) out the door of the suite.

"Mrrrraaa. What just happened?" Sam asked, digging a single claw even deeper into my arm. "Who does that blowhard think he is? Just because he's the size of a small planet—no, I take that back, a huge planet—he thinks he can boss everyone around. Retired sheriff, my eye. Did anybody get a good look at that badge he flashed? Probably came out of a box of Cracker Jack."

"It looked real enough," said Clarence.

"Well, I'm not giving up," said Sam. "There's more holes in this case than a trainload of Swiss cheese."

"What can we do?" I asked.

Sam jumped down to the floor. "Back to the dormitory. I think best in my own bed. With a bowl of fresh Jersey cream. And a can of Sail On sardines. If only someone cared enough about me to provide those two simple necessities of life."

Don't Call Me Samantha
THE ALMOST ENTIRELY TRUE
AUTOBIOGRAPHY OF LANTERN SAM

A Taste of Adventure (and Sardines)

While the two arrow holes in my neck healed, I began to think that perhaps it was time for me to see a bit of the world outside of Linesville, Pennsylvania. After all, I'd already been squashed by a thousand pounds of dairy cow and shish kebabed by one of the most dangerous creatures I know—a boy—and I was still two months away from my first birthday. How much more dangerous could the outside world be?

I've never been a big fan of the long goodbye, so I strolled out of the barn before the morning milking one fine September day without a look back at my still-sleeping siblings, and headed north. Why north? Simple. I'd heard rumors of a lake so big that you couldn't see across it, and boats overflowing with fresh-caught perch and walleye. Lake Erie: it sounded like heaven.

It didn't take me long to figure out that traveling on paw was for the birds, so to speak. Luckily, I met a grizzled old tabby named Butch—originally from a town in northern Ontario—who introduced me to the world of train travel. Together we hopped a Bessemer & Lake Erie coal train bound for Ashtabula, and we were treated to a meal of canned tuna and slightly sour milk in the caboose by a conductor named Charlie Nockwood—Clarence's older brother!

When we got to Ashtabula, Butch pointed me in the direction of the piers where the fishing boats docked and sent me on my way with a single piece of advice: "Cats and boats don't mix, Sam. Hang out all you want and enjoy the fresh fish, but whatever you do, don't ever step aboard one of those death traps. It's like being in prison, but with a much better chance of drowning. No boats. Promise?"

I promised.

Yes, I broke that promise—but to be fair, it was unintentional. I swear.

The weather had turned unseasonably chilly, and I was sauntering down the pier where the fishermen clean their catch, hoping to snag a few scraps for myself. Through a porthole of a tidy, well-cared-for fishing boat, I spied a kerosene lantern burning brightly. I thought about Butch's warning, but I convinced myself that I would go aboard only long enough to warm up, maybe find a little something to eat, and then plant my feet back on terra firma, where cats belong. Besides, the boat was named *Susie G*, and I had a sister Susie. Surely that was a good sign. And so, in a weak moment brought on by the cold and an empty stomach, I leaped from the pier onto the deck. I poked around the companionway for a while, watching and listening for signs of life below deck.

When I was sure the coast was clear, I climbed down the stairs into the cabin, where the smells of fish and mildewed foul-weather gear mingled irresistibly. I searched that boat from bow to stern without turning up so much as a crumb. Cold and discouraged, I curled up next to the kerosene lantern for a short nap before moving on.

The next thing I remember was the sound of feet hitting the deck right above my head and the engine roaring to life. The kerosene lantern must have burned itself out hours earlier because it was icy cold to the touch and I couldn't stop shivering. Outside the porthole it was still dark, and by the time I was awake enough to get a good look, the *Susie G* was on her way, slipping under the drawbridge and heading out into the lake!

Unsure of how the crew would react to finding a stranger aboard, I shook off the cold and the sleep and searched for a place to hide until we returned to shore. And I almost succeeded.

Almost.

Above the counter where I had spent the night was a cubbyhole full of canned goods. Someone had left the door open an inch or two, just enough for me to squeeze inside. I crawled into the back corner and wedged myself in place as the *Susie* G began to rock back and forth in the waves. And I would have been fine if the weather had cooperated a little more.

The wind began to pick up the moment we cleared the breakwater in the harbor, and the waves began to grow higher and higher, until they were crashing over the bow and the little *Susie* G was tossed this way and that, over and over. Secure in my cubby, I closed my eyes and prayed that the crew knew what they were doing.

"Nasty out there," a man's voice said.

"Nor'easter," said another. "Three days of this. The fishing will be lousy and the captain will be grouchy."

Just then the *Susie* G fell off the top of an especially large wave and landed with a shudder, causing all the cans in my cubby to fly toward the door, crashing through it—with me right behind! Down I went in a cascade of soup cans, landing on the back of a crew member who had momentarily lost his footing.

"Hey! What's going—" he shouted.

"Where did *that* come from?" the other asked, pointing at me.

Before the first one could answer, however, we hit another wave and the last can in the cabinet flew out the open door as if it had been shot from a cannon and hit me square between the eyes. The last thing I saw before everything went black was a bright red label decorated with a tiny fish and the words *Sail On Sardines.*

When I came to, my head was throbbing and it took me a few seconds to remember where I was. A bearded, scruffy man in blue coveralls smiled when I opened my eyes.

"I'll be darned," he said. "You're right, Irv. She's not dead."

"Not yet, anyway," said the other. "Just don't let Jim see her. He hates cats almost as much as he hates his ex-wife."

"What should we do with it?"

"Mrrrraaa," I said.

The second man felt my ribs. "Why don't you give her some of those sardines? Looks like she hasn't eaten in a while. You know, she's sort of *like* a sardine—all skin and bones."

It seems hard to believe now, but until that moment, I had never even heard of sardines—the Dillys were strictly meat-and-potatoes people. So I watched with fascination as the bearded one twisted the key around and around, finally lifting the lid to reveal the irresistible scent that has haunted me ever since. He set the tin on the floorboards, and I paused for a moment to savor that delicious smell and then took my first bite of sardine.

It was almost my last, as well.

The two men immediately backed away from me as Jim Elbert, the captain of the *Susie G*, clomped down the companionway stairs. I was too busy inhaling the heady odor of sardine to notice.

"What—in—the—name—of—Sam—Hill—is—going—on?" he demanded. "Who brought that . . . cat . . . on my boat? And you're feeding it my food?"

He didn't wait for an explanation. Roughly grabbing me by the scruff of the neck, he marched back up the stairs and, without another word, heaved me over the stern of the *Susie G* and into storm-tossed Lake Erie. As I landed with a splash and found myself underwater for the first time in my life, Butch's words echoed in my head: *Cats and boats don't mix.*

Another myth about cats is that we're not good swimmers. Not true. We can swim like crazy when we have to, and being thrown off a boat seven or eight miles from shore is a perfect example of one of those "have to" situations. From the top of a giant wave, I spotted the shore in the distance and started to paddle in that direction. I knew that my making it back to shore was a long shot at best, but I had to give it a try.

I was tired, cold, and hungry—I'd barely gotten one bite of sardines down when my breakfast was so rudely interrupted. I needed another miracle, and I got one.

Okay, maybe *miracle* is too strong a word, but that wooden packing crate that floated past a few minutes later certainly was welcome. I climbed aboard, sunk my claws into the soft wood, and held on for dear life as the wind howled and waves crashed all around me, pushing me toward the shore.

I drifted like that for several hours. The entrance to the harbor was still a long, long way off, and I grew more desperate for a nap by the minute. Midafternoon, the sun finally broke through the clouds, and I spied a sailboat a mile or so out. I watched as the distance between us closed; it was headed right for me. A lone man was on deck, but as he got closer and closer, I realized that he didn't see me or my crate—in fact, I was pretty sure he was asleep at the tiller!

"Mrrraaa!" I shouted, but the sound was swallowed up by the wind and waves.

As I prepared myself for the collision, the bow of the sailboat dipped way down into the wave I was riding, spearing the crate and lifting it clear of the water with me still somehow (miraculously?) attached. The sound woke the sailor, who left the tiller and rushed forward, snagging me with one hand and pushing the crate away from his boat with the other.

"Hey there, little lady," he said. "What's a nice kitty like you doing out on a day like this?"

"Mrrraaa," I said. "Please, mister, for the love of Pete, just dry me off and give me something to eat."

He gave me a strange look, and later on I realized that he was probably the first human to hear me. Down in the cabin, he rubbed me dry with a towel and then . . . well, then he did something really special: he opened a can of sardines for me. They weren't the Sail On brand, but they weren't half bad.

His name was Walt, and I probably would have stuck with him if it weren't for one important fact: he *lived* on that little sailboat, and I had decided that on the topic of cats and boats, Butch was definitely right. And so, when we got to shore, we went our separate ways, with Walt continuing on to Cleveland and points beyond, and me staying on in Ashtabula. I had some unfinished business to take care of.

From the warmth of the drawbridge control tower, I watched as the *Susie* G returned to port three days later. Captain Elbert growled at his crew as they unloaded the paltry catch, and then he snarled some more when they took too long to scrub the decks. Finally, he pulled the main hatch closed and drove away in his beat-up Chevrolet.

Under cover of darkness, I went to work. I had spent the previous day learning a little about boats, you see. I learned that every boat has valves that are used to let water *into* the boat—for cleaning up, and filling tanks, and so on—and I learned how to open those valves.

You can probably guess how the rest of this story goes.

The next morning, Captain Elbert found the *Susie G* sitting hard on the bottom of the harbor with only her cabin top visible. As he ranted and raved, something on the dock got his attention. A small piece of paper, weighed down by a rock, flapped in the breeze: a Sail On sardines label.

Chapter 4

S am opened his eyes after fifteen minutes of "deep thinking." He sniffed at the bowl of cream that Clarence had placed next to him, turning up his nose at it. *"All right, let's start with what we know."*

"Looks like Ellie Strasbourg was kidnapped by a traveling salesman," said Clarence.

"You're half right," Sam grumbled. *"Which is about average for you. I'll grant you that Ellie Strasbourg has been kidnapped. As for the salesman . . . are you sure this is the only cream they have? Maybe there's some Jersey cream left over from the last trip."*

Clarence sighed. "Yes, Sam, I'm sure. That's the only cream on board. Can we please move on? Because somebody certainly wants us to think this salesman's involved."

"That's not the same as knowing, though," argued Sam. *"We*

know that somebody emptied a salesman's case in the baggage compartment. And left behind a handkerchief that smells like chloroform, or at least what I suppose chloroform smells like. And that there was a salesman, or someone pretending to be a salesman, in another compartment."

"Where there was a picture of Ellie and her mother from last fall. And a ransom note," I added. "Sure looks to me like the salesman did it."

Ignoring my contribution to the discussion, Sam scratched under his chin with his back leg and moved on to the next topic. "Henry, where was Ellie when you saw her last?"

"In the club car. I left her there while I ran to the observation car to get my sketchbook. When I got back, she was gone."

"How long was that?" Sam asked.

"Only a minute. I was counting, because she said she would wait for exactly one minute."

"And when you returned and saw that she was gone, what did you do?"

I closed my eyes, remembering. "I talked to a man in the club car for . . . about ten seconds."

"What man? What did he look like? What did he say . . . exactly?"

"Um, he was just a man. He was wearing a suit, a gray suit. He was old, like thirty."

"Thirty, old! What does that make me? I must be down-right ancient," said Clarence.

"Prehistoric, basically," Sam said wryly.

"He teased me about looking for my girlfriend," I added. "Then he said that Ellie went toward the front of the train. On the way past my mother, I stopped to ask her if she'd seen Ellie, but she didn't even know her. Then I came straight here."

"So, in total there were two . . . maybe three minutes between your last sight of Ellie and when you found me," said Sam. *"And when you got here, was the curtain open or closed?"*

"It was closed. No, that's not right. It was halfway open." I reached up and pulled the curtain partially shut. "About like this." ·

"That's right," said Sam. *"And then you stayed with me until the train stopped in Albany."*

"Did anybody go past you into the baggage area?" Clarence asked.

I shook my head. "No. I'm positive. I would remember."

"So, Sam, how about you? What about the two or three minutes right before Henry showed up?" said Clarence. "You say the curtain was half open. Did you see anybody?"

"Yes," said Sam. *"A porter, going in to get baggage ready for the Albany stop. It was Donnie, the one with all the muscles. And that's it. I never saw—or heard—Ellie or any other passengers."*

"Sorry, Sam, old boy, but I'm afraid the sworn testimony of a cat doesn't count for much. Not everyone is as enlightened as Henry and I," said Clarence. "I suppose I should talk to Donnie, anyway. Maybe he noticed something. At the very least we'll get a description of the salesman, and we can send it to the police in Albany."

My head was spinning as I tried to keep up. "But . . . if Ellie didn't go in . . . and nobody moved the trunk *out* . . . then how did the kidnapper . . . And where is Ellie?"

Sam squeezed his eyes shut. *"Shhh. I'm* thinking."

"It's best if we leave him alone for a while to think," said Clarence, pulling the curtain closed.

"Before we go, I . . . um, there's something else I forgot to mention. Something Ellie said. I didn't really believe her, but she was sure there were *criminals* on the train. Supposedly, she recognized them from their pictures in the post office—a man and a woman."

"How sure was she?" Clarence asked.

"She *said* she was positive. She swears that she has a photographic memory. But she couldn't remember their names, just their faces. When I asked her what they looked like, she said they were ordinary. That's what we were talking about that first time we met you. She thought we would be famous if we caught them. But we never got the chance to talk about them again."

"Mrrraaa," said Sam, opening the eye in the center of his "patch." *"Criminals, you say. Plural. Most interesting."*

Judge Ambrose, who had taken over the back end of the observation car for his investigation, chewed noisily on a soggy cigar and sneered at me the way I imagined he sneered at career criminals in his courtroom.

"And you're certain—absolutely certain—that the last place you saw Miss Strasbourg was in the club car," he said after listening to my story.

"Yes, sir." It was killing me to address him as *sir,* but I could hear my father's voice in my head reminding me that there would be times in my life when I would have to swallow my pride.

"I'm having a hard time understanding one thing, Mr. . . . Shipley, is it? Maybe you can explain to me what a girl like Ellie Strasbourg was doing with the likes of you. You've seen how her family lives. Now take a good look at yourself. I'll bet your dear old mother makes all your clothes for you, doesn't she? And those shoes—how many times have they been resoled?"

I shifted nervously in my seat. Ambrose was right on both counts—lucky guess, the big baboon. Mother *did* make our clothes, and she was proud of it. My shoes were hand-me-downs from my cousin Arnold, who was a year older.

"You see what I'm getting at, don't you?" Ambrose continued. "It seems hard to believe that she would *want* to spend time with a boy so . . . well, like you. Why were you pestering her? Did someone put you up to it? Are you involved in this? What did they offer you?"

"What? No!" I protested. "I wasn't bothering her. We were friends. For your information, I was minding my own business when *she* started talking to *me*. She told me that she was going to Conneaut Lake Park to ride the Blue Streak. She wasn't bragging or anything—she just, you know, talked . . . a *lot*. She told me that there were criminals on board."

"Criminals!" said Ambrose, spitting slimy bits of tobacco into my face. "Come now, surely she was pulling your leg."

I wiped the spit and tobacco from my face and shook my head firmly. "She recognized their pictures from the post office. She said she checked the photos there every week. It was a man and a woman."

Ambrose leaned in and asked, "Did you ever see these so-called criminals?"

"No. We were going to look for them when she . . . disappeared."

"Did she describe them to you?"

"Not really. She just said they were ordinary."

Ambrose eyed me even more skeptically. "So, these

ordinary-looking criminals, who are wanted by the FBI, just walked up to the counter in Grand Central Station and bought tickets on the Shoreliner—that's what you're saying?"

"No, that's what *Ellie* said."

"I'm done with you for now," said Ambrose, dismissing me with a wave. "I'll probably need to talk to you again."

"Gee, I can't wait," I muttered. "I just love it when people spit tobacco juice on me."

While the Shoreliner raced westward at sixty miles per hour, Judge Ambrose questioned everyone who had seen Ellie, along with a few others who "looked suspicious" to him. Then, after examining the baggage room and the compartment where the salesman had left the ransom note and other clues behind, he invited Clarence to the observation car, where, he said, he would announce his findings.

Clarence joined Mrs. Strasbourg, her maid Julia, and Reverend Perfiddle in the seats at the back of the train, which the judge and the good reverend had cleared. Sam and I hid in the vestibule between cars, waiting for the judge to turn his back to us. The moment he did, we scampered down the aisle and ducked behind the bar that divided the rear half of the car.

"After investigating this incident thoroughly," the judge

began, "it is abundantly clear what happened, ma'am. Apparently, your daughter wandered up into the dormitory area, which is in the car directly behind the locomotive. She was, as I understand it, going there in order to visit the conductor's *cat*, which remains on board with the conductor—against regulations, I believe. But that is another matter, for another day. The safe return of Ellie Strasbourg must be our number one priority. I believe that this traveling salesman—we don't know his name yet—was lying in wait for her somewhere nearby. It would seem that he surprised her as she was petting the cat and took her into the baggage area, which is separated from the dormitory area by a kind of cloth wall, with a door that snaps shut."

Judge Ambrose produced the handkerchief that I had discovered from his pocket and continued. "He then used *this*—soaked in ether, or perhaps chloroform—to subdue her, and then put her into the sample case that he had emptied. When the train arrived in Albany, the porters unknowingly helped him with the case, and off he went. I sent a telegram to the police there, and they'll be checking the roads between Albany and Dunkirk, but it's a long shot at best that they'll turn anything up. The kidnapper has a good head start."

Once again, Mrs. Strasbourg wailed loudly. "Where would they take her? Will they harm her? There must be *something* we can do. I can't just sit here and wait—I'll lose my mind with worry."

Clarence did his best to calm her. "Don't you worry, Mrs. Strasbourg. Your little Ellie will be fine, mark my words. And the police will catch the people who are responsible."

With the slimy stub of a cigar clenched in his teeth, Judge Ambrose twirled the ends of his mustache between his fingers. "Yes, yes, indeed they will. But you're right, Mrs. Strasbourg. We need to talk about what to do next. With the kidnapper and your daughter already off the train, and no police at hand, I don't see that we have much choice here. We need to make preparations to follow the kidnapper's instructions and pay the ransom, I'm afraid."

"Whatever you think is best, Judge," said Mrs. Strasbourg. "I don't care about anything except getting my Ellie back."

"Pardon me, *Mr.* Ambrose," said Clarence, "but don't you think it's a little soon to be talking about that? It's still a long way to the Dunkirk station, and, well, I'm not sure that all the questions have been answered. I'll admit that I'm no expert, but there's still a great deal that we can— and *should*—do."

"Way to go, Clarence!" said Sam. *"Don't let him bully you. It's your train, after all. He's just a passenger. A planet-sized passenger, but still just a passenger."*

Judge Ambrose scoffed. "What would you have me do, Mr. Nockwood?"

Reverend Perfiddle, who had been listening intently, lit another cigarette and addressed Mrs. Strasbourg directly. "My dear Mrs. Strasbourg, I'm afraid that Judge Ambrose is right. In times like these, you can't afford to quibble. I don't mean to sound callous, but your daughter's life is at stake here. The conductor, Mr. . . . . Nockley, was it?"

"Nock*wood,*" said Clarence.

"Yes, yes. My apologies. Interesting name. As I was saying, Mr. Nockwood seems to be forgetting what is on the line here."

Clarence stood up in protest and pointed his finger at the judge. "You've only talked to a handful of people on the train—there still may be someone who saw, or heard, something important. Someone who saw the salesman talking to another passenger. For instance, the young man that you spoke to—"

"The Shipley kid? Why should we believe anything he says?" the judge blustered. "Boy like that, he'd say anything to get his name in the papers, I'll bet."

Reverend Perfiddle touched Mrs. Strasbourg on her arm. "The boy's story is a bit fishy. I wasn't present for the interview, but Judge Ambrose filled me in on the important details. Claims to have been a friend of your daughter's."

"A bit *fishy!*" I hissed at Sam, struggling to keep my voice down. "Say anything to get my name in the papers! I never—"

"*Easy, kid,*" said Sam.

Clarence, biting his lip in frustration, sat back down. He took a deep, calming breath and continued. "Well, then, what about the criminals that she recognized? Don't you think that could be important? Have you even considered the possibility that she was right?"

Mrs. Strasbourg pulled her arm away from Reverend Perfiddle. "Wh-what . . . criminals? Ellie recognized some-one? How? Who?"

"According to young Mr. Shipley," Ambrose said, "your daughter told him that she recognized two criminals, a man and a woman, from their photographs in the post of-fice. I think he's lying, trying to put us off the trail of the real kidnapper. It's obvious that he's protecting someone. As a judge, I see cases like this all the time. Young man from . . . well, the wrong side of the tracks meets a pretty little girl from a good family . . ."

I couldn't believe what I was hearing. That behemoth was accusing me of helping the kidnappers! Just as I was about to leave my hiding place and defend my honor, Sam reached up and put a paw on my leg, extending a single claw into the first few layers of skin. *"Don't. It's not worth it. Not yet, anyway."*

"Now wait just a second," said Clarence. "Surely you don't suspect the boy merely because he's not from a wealthy family. And I don't think it's fair—or accurate—to say that he's from 'the wrong side of the tracks.' He simply reported what his friend told him. We should be praising him for coming forward, rather than questioning his character."

"Perhaps," said Ambrose, chomping on his soggy cigar.

"But what if Ellie was right," Mrs. Strasbourg argued, "and she *did* recognize these people? She does have a remarkable memory. Perhaps she did see a picture of them somewhere. One of them might still be on the train. I think that Mr. Nockwood is right. We have to keep looking. Please, Judge Ambrose—for Ellie."

Clarence nodded, pleased that she was taking a firm stand.

Julia looked at Mrs. Strasbourg. "Excuse me, ma'am."

"What is it, Julia? Do you know something?"

"Yes, ma'am. It's true . . . what the judge said about Ellie seeing the pictures at the post office. I'm sorry; I let her go inside every week, right after her piano lesson. She said it was for a game she was playing. I didn't think there was any harm in it." She started to cry, and Mrs. Strasbourg touched her gently on the arm.

Clarence checked his pocket watch and turned to Ambrose. "There—you see? You can't ignore what the boy said. Dinner service will begin soon. I can arrange to have you seated at table three. You'll be able to see everyone who comes into the dining car. I'd be happy to find you a pad of paper to take notes."

Ambrose glared at Clarence. "To the dining car, then," he grumbled.

Despite Clarence's best efforts to keep Ellie's disappearance quiet, rumors about a missing rich girl from the deluxe Commodore Perry suite spread like a grassfire from one end of the train to the other. By the time passengers returned to their rooms to dress for dinner, virtually everyone on the Shoreliner had heard *something* about a kidnapping, and those who were parents demanded to speak to the conductor about what was being done to ensure their children's safety.

Clarence knew that he needed to reassure the passengers, especially those traveling with children. In order to keep the situation under control, he and the two porters he trusted most set out to knock on every compartment door and explain what had happened.

"*You do what you have to do,*" Sam told Clarence. "*Henry and I'll be snooping on His Immenseness.*"

When no one was looking, Clarence led Sam and me into the dining car, where the upright piano had been pushed against a wall to make room for another table. Clarence pulled it out a few inches and motioned for us to squeeze behind it.

"*Mrrraaa. Not much room back here,*" complained Sam.

"What about me?" I said. "I'm a lot bigger than you."

"Are you going to be all right?" Clarence asked.

"*There's only one problem,*" said Sam. "*We can hear people but we can't see them. How are we supposed to know who's talking?*"

"How about a big vase of flowers to hide behind?" Clarence suggested. "That's what they always do in the pictures. Let me see what I can find."

"*While you're at it, how about a little something to eat? I'm famished,*" said Sam. "*What's that I smell, pork chops?*"

"You're just going to have to wait."

"*Oh, fine. You'll get the boy genius everything he asks for, but I ask for one little pork chop and suddenly you're too busy. If I die of starvation back here, please don't tell my mother I went like this. She had such great expectations where I was concerned. It would break her poor, weak heart.*"

"Oh no," I said, suddenly remembering the promise I'd made to my mother.

"You have to go to the bathroom, don't you?" Sam asked. *"I told you to go before we came back here."*

"It's not that. My mother—she'll be looking for me. She said she wanted to treat us to a nice meal in the dining car for a change, instead of stale sandwiches."

"Leave it to me," said Clarence. "I'll take care of everything. Now, shhh! Someone's coming."

It didn't take us long to figure out who that someone was, even though we couldn't see anything from behind the piano. The heels of a pair of sturdy men's shoes (custom built in a factory in Hoboken, New Jersey, to withstand forces no ordinary shoe could handle) *clack*ed loudly, and the floorboards beneath them creaked in protest with every step. When Judge Ambrose finally came to a stop and lowered himself onto a chair, its wooden frame groaned so noisily that I cringed, waiting for its imminent collapse.

"Fee-fie-fo-fum," said Sam. *"I smell the blood of a half-ton bum."*

I had to cover my mouth to keep myself from laughing out loud.

"Waiter!" shouted the judge. "Bourbon, and make it snappy."

When the waiter returned less than a minute later, Ambrose complained about how long it had taken and told him to leave the bottle.

"*Glad to see he's taking this investigation so seriously,*" said Sam as we listened in awe to the *glug-glug-glug* of liquor splashing into a glass.

And Sam's eyes were wider than mine when, seconds later, Ambrose slammed that glass down onto the table and refilled it!

"He drinks like the sailors on Father's ship," I noted. "Father says they have hollow legs."

"*Based on the sound that chair made when he sat in it, I don't think any part of him is hollow,*" said Sam.

Clarence walked past, placing a vase filled with colorful flowers on top of the piano before checking up on Judge Ambrose.

"Everything all right here, Judge? You should be able to observe everyone on board from this table. Sooner or later, everyone will come in for something to eat."

Judge Ambrose grumbled something unintelligible, and then added, "Complete waste of time if you ask me. At least the whisky's good. Since this is an official investigation, you'll see to it that I'm not charged for it, I'm sure. Now, how about some dinner? Three or four of those pork chops ought to do the trick."

"I'll send a waiter right over," said Clarence. "I've been telling the passengers that you'll be here, and that you'll want to talk to some of them."

"Correction: I don't *want* to talk to any of them. I'm only doing this for Mrs. Strasbourg's sake."

I peeked through the wilted flowers in time to see Clarence turn away from the judge as two women, obviously sisters, approached his table. I've never been very good at guessing ages, but I thought they were probably in their late thirties, with nearly identical hairdos and long dresses that matched the flowers right in front of my nose.

"Excuse us, Judge Ambrose," said one. "Do you have a moment?"

"Why certainly, ladies," he said, turning on a kind of greasy, sickening charm that I felt sure *anyone* could see through. "Won't you sit? Would you like a drink?"

"Oh, no, we don't wish to disturb your dinner," said the slightly-more-brunette sister. "My name is Gladys Henshaw, and this is my sister Gwendolyn. We, er, I may have heard something important. I didn't think anything of it at the time, but now, with what's happened . . . we . . ."

"Yeeessss?" The judge leaned in, his forehead deeply furrowed.

"He looks worried," I whispered to Sam.

Gladys Henshaw continued. "The conductor mentioned a man, a traveling salesman of some kind, who may be involved with the little girl's disappearance. You see, my sister and I were having a cup of tea in the club car not long after we departed from New York, and I believe that we may have spoken to such a man."

"He was very polite," said Gwendolyn. "He said that he was a marble salesman, and he was on his way to Albany for the biggest deal of his life. He was going to get the contract for the new courthouse."

Gladys shivered. "He was going to make a *killing*—that was the word he used. It gives me a chill now, just thinking of it. If everything went according to his plan, he would make more money in one day than most people make in a lifetime."

"But you see, Judge Ambrose," Gwendolyn said, "there is no new courthouse in Albany. My best friend, Maryanne Hawthorp, works in the existing courthouse, and believe me, she would know if something like that were happening. She is the nosiest person you'd ever want to meet."

"I see," said the judge. "That's very interesting, and possibly quite helpful, ladies. Thank you for bringing it to my attention."

"There's one more thing," said Gladys. "He made a point of saying that he usually stayed at the State Street Hotel when he was in Albany, but this time he was going to treat himself and stay at the Fitzgerald."

"That's the nicest hotel in the city. He might be there right now!" said Gwendolyn.

Judge Ambrose scribbled something on his notepad and thanked the ladies again for their help. "I'll look into this myself. The Fitzgerald, you say."

"What do you think?" I whispered to Sam.

"Sounds to me like the salesman was trying to impress the two ladies," said Sam. *"Remember what the porter said about him. That he was a real smooth talker. I think the whole courthouse story was a lie."*

"What about Ellie? Did he kidnap her?"

"Write a note to Clarence, and tell him to send a telegram to Albany. Somebody should at least check the State Street Hotel for our friend Romeo."

"Don't you mean the Fitzgerald?"

"Ha! I have friends in Albany, and from what they've told me, the Fitz is a first-class operation. The bellmen there are so snobby they'd never even let a salesman like Romeo into the lobby—except maybe to polish the marble floors in the middle of the night."

I dug the stub of a pencil out of my pocket, quickly scribbled the note on a scrap of paper, and handed it to Clarence on his next pass by the piano. When I looked up, a man and a woman were preparing to sit at the lone table between the judge's table and the piano. As the man helped his wife into her chair, I recognized him immediately as the man in the gray suit—the one from the club car who had teased me about Ellie. The woman, I noticed immediately, wore a scarf tied around her head and fashionable dark glasses, even though she was inside a train car *and* the sun was hidden behind clouds.

Sam noticed the same thing. *"Now, there's somebody who doesn't want to be recognized. Look how she's sitting, bent over, hiding behind her menu. The scarf, the glasses—I wonder what her story is. She's up to no good—you can count on that."*

"You're a very suspicious person, er, cat," I said.

"In my line of work, you have to be. Tell me, what else do you see when you really look at them?"

I watched them for a while, then shrugged. "I don't know—other than the sunglasses, they look kind of ordinary to me."

"Look at their hands. He can't stop fiddling with his wedding ring, and she can't stop looking at hers. What does that tell you?"

"They're married?"

"Mrrrraa. Maybe they are, maybe they aren't, but they're certainly not used to wearing those rings. They could be newlyweds—after all, he did pull the chair out for her. Husbands don't do that for long."

"My father still does it for my mother," I said. It was true; Captain Shipley was an old-fashioned gentleman, through and through.

"Well, he's the exception to the rule."

As Sam and I watched, the man reached across the table

and took the woman's hand in his. He spoke softly: "Stop worrying. Everything's going to work out perfectly. We're going to get away with it, at least until—"

"Until someone recognizes me," said the woman, slinking even lower into her seat. "If word gets out, those vultures will be waiting for us when we get off the train. You saw the way that girl looked at me—I'm telling you, she *knew*. And then there's our friend with the bird's nest on her head. It's no accident that *she's* here."

"As soon as we're done with dinner," said the man, "we'll go back to our room and stay there. It's too late for the little girl to say anything, and don't worry about our friend with the hat. I'll take care of her."

Don't Call Me Samantha
THE ALMOST ENTIRELY TRUE
AUTOBIOGRAPHY OF LANTERN SAM

A Jealous Tom, a Fierce Rooster, and Me

Her name was Marmalade and she was nothing but trouble from the moment I laid eyes on her. She was a round-faced tabby with long legs and a voice that made me go weak in the knees. The first time I saw her, she was on the roof of Fagin's Place, a hole-in-the-wall bar down by the Cuyahoga River.

"Rrroooowww," she said. "Hey there, handsome."

I looked around, wondering who she was talking to.

"I'm talking to you, Calico. You new in town?"

Back on the Dilly farm, Mom had warned me about girls like Marmalade, and I should have just kept walking. But for the second time in less than a week, I ignored the advice of an older and wiser cat. I couldn't help myself; Marmalade was a knockout.

"Came in on the train today," I said. "From Ashta—"

She cut me off. "Why don't you come up here so I can get a closer look at you. I've never seen a boy calico. Go around to the side. There's a stack of old beer kegs in front of the truck that's parked there. If you climb up those, you can jump onto the roof of the truck, and then . . . you'll see. It's easy from there."

I hesitated for a moment and the first few drops of rain splashed onto the pavement at my feet.

"It's dry up here," said Marmalade, ducking under an over-hang. "You don't want to get wet, do you?"

"Not really," I said. I'd had enough water for a lifetime.

I climbed up the stack of kegs, then leaped onto the roof of the truck.

"Whatever you do, don't fall into the back of that truck," she warned.

In the bed of the truck were a dozen wooden cages, each with three or four chickens inside, clucking and cooing.

I had spent time around chickens back on the farm in Linesville, so I wasn't too worried. "I'm not afraid of chickens," I said, jumping from the truck roof to a tree branch and then onto the roof next to Marmalade.

She looked me up and down, frowning. "Rrowww. Why, you're just a baby. What are you, a whole year old?"

"Not quite."

"And I'll bet this is your first time in the big city, right?"

I nodded.

"What's your name?"

"Sam."

"Well, Sam, it's your lucky day. My name is Marmalade and I'm going to show you all the best spots in Cleveland. Do you like oysters, Sam? Because I know a place where—"

Without warning, a bolt of lightning tore the sky open directly above us, blinding me temporarily. Fagin's Place shook beneath my feet, and every bit of my hair stood on end from all the static electricity in the air. When I was finally able to see again, a gray tom, three times my size, stood between Marmalade and me. To this day, I have no idea where he came from; at the time, I was convinced that he rode in on the back of the lightning bolt.

"I thought you were out of town," purred Marmalade.

"Obviously," the tom growled. "Who's the shrimp?"

"This is Sam. He's new in town. Sam, meet Tom."

A tomcat named Tom? How *creative*, I thought.

"Nice to, er, meet you, Tom," I stammered.

Tom circled me silently, a lion sizing up his prey.

"Easy, Tom," said Marmalade. "Please don't hurt him. Nothing happened. He's practically a kitten."

"Just a scratch," said Tom. "A little something to remember me by."

I thought I was ready, but the truth is that I never even saw it coming. I'd done plenty of fighting with my brothers and sisters, but they all had one thing in common: they were all right-pawed. Tom, it turned out, was a southpaw.

And what a paw! The first swipe took a notch out of my right ear, and the second spun me around so hard I sailed off the roof, bounced once on the top of the truck, and then landed with a thump in the back, right smack in the middle of the chicken cages. At the moment I hit the truck bed, the owner hit the ignition, and the engine sputtered for a second before springing to life. As we bounced down the alley behind Fagin's Place, I heard Tom laughing from the roof above me.

"Get up, Sam!" cried Marmalade. "You have to get out of there before—"

It was already too late. I was about to discover why the owner of the truck wasn't worried about anyone trying to steal his chickens. (I know what you're thinking: why does anyone drive around with chickens in the first place? I still don't know the answer to that question.)

No matter how tough you think you are, you do *not*

want—ever—to find yourself between a very protective rooster and a bunch of hens. Now, before you laugh, I'll just mention that the rooster outweighed me by a dozen pounds, and on top of that, he had the advantage of surprise. The monster came out of nowhere—a spinning, kicking, pecking, slashing, feathered blur—and I was bruised and bloodied in a matter of seconds. I got in a couple of decent hits, ending up with a paw full of feathers at one point, and he backed off momentarily in order to regroup. I wasn't about to stick around for part two, though, so I climbed up the tailgate and jumped.

In the midst of the teeming rain and all that rooster fury, however, I hadn't realized that the truck had sped up to about thirty-five miles an hour, so when I hit the road, I skidded along the edge of the pavement, desperately trying to bring myself to a stop. All my claws were worn down to the nubs and one was yanked out completely, never to grow back, leaving me with only seventeen. (Like most cats, I started out with eighteen, not twenty, in case you're wondering.)

But my night wasn't over yet.

Maybe if I hadn't lost that claw, I would have been able to stop a few feet shorter. Two, three feet—that's all the difference I needed. Instead, a river of rainwater swept me straight into a storm sewer! When my head finally bobbed back to the surface, I found myself floating down the rapids below street level, getting dunked by a waterfall every time I passed under another drain.

I continued like that for probably half a mile in utter darkness, cursing my luck, a cat named Marmalade, and a watchrooster with an exceptionally bad attitude. My hopes lifted when I finally saw a speck of light in the distance: the end of the ride! The pipe ended suddenly, firing a furry, soaked-to-the-bone cannonball into Cleveland Harbor.

Using my last bit of energy, I swam back to shore and managed to pull myself up onto a dock, much to the surprise of the sailor who had tied up his boat for the night.

"Hey, I know you," said Walt, who probably recognized me because I looked exactly like I had the first time we met. "Again? I thought cats hated the water. Let me get you dried off and find you something to eat. Do you like *chicken?*"

I shuddered, picturing the face of the crazed rooster who tried to kill me. "Mrrraaa. It just became my second favorite food."

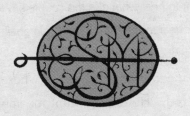

Chapter 5

I nudged Sam. "Did he just say what I think he said?" My already overactive imagination was churning and sputtering: *Why* was it too late for the little girl to say something? Was he talking about Ellie? What had he done to her? And *how*, exactly, was the man going to "take care of" the lady in the hat?

While those questions and a thousand others were spinning wildly through my brain, Clarence unexpectedly touched me on the shoulder. I gasped so loudly that we were all sure everyone in the dining car heard.

"Dinnertime, Henry," Clarence whispered. "Your table will be ready in a few minutes." He moved the piano just enough for me to crawl out.

"Hear anything interesting?" Clarence asked Sam as he pushed the piano back into place.

"Plenty. I want to hear what else this couple has to say. And then you need to get me into the salesman's cabin again—there's something I need to see."

Clarence glanced over at the judge, whose nose seemed to be glowing red. "He doesn't want me snooping around anymore, but you know what—it's still my train."

"That's the spirit," said Sam. "Besides, after all that booze, it would take a bulldozer to move His Enormousness."

"Uh-oh, you spoke too soon. Here he comes," said Clarence, pretending to be busy wiping dust from the top of the piano. I ducked around the corner, out of sight.

"Who the devil are you talking to?" Judge Ambrose demanded. He walked around the piano and looked behind it. "Is that cat in here? Get him out—now! Mr. Nockwood. My daughter and I are highly allergic to cats, especially common alley cats like that one, and we will not be subjected to such bothersome complications. You leave me no choice, sir. I shall write to the president of the railroad and inform him of the less-than-satisfactory conditions aboard this train."

With that, the judge took a cane from a man sitting at a nearby table and began to poke it in Sam's direction.

A growl rose from deep within Sam as he dodged the end of the cane. *"Hsssttt!"* he screamed, and spat.

"Stop!" cried Clarence. "You'll hurt him, you— I'll take care of it, *Mr.* Ambrose. Go, Sam, run!"

Sam bolted past Clarence and the judge, then scooted through the dining car and into the sleepers, with me a few steps behind.

Mother stood in the aisle next to our section with her back to me, gathering Jessica into her arms before heading into the dining car. Jessica's eyes grew wide with excitement as we raced past. "Kitty!"

"What?" Mother asked, but by the time she turned to look, Sam and I were long gone.

Five minutes later Sam, Clarence, and I were standing in front of the compartment that had been occupied by the marble salesman. The hair down the center of Sam's back still hadn't settled into place, and his tail was three times its normal size.

"A cane! Did you see the look in his eyes? He was trying to kill me! And on top of that, he insulted me and my family. Common alley cat, indeed. He is going to live to regret that, mark my words. If he so much as turns his back to me, I'm going to shred him into a pile of ribbon the size of the city dump in Erie. He messed with the wrong calico."

"Easy, Sam," said Clarence. "Remember what they say about revenge."

"I think the Greek poet Homer said that it is sweeter than flowing honey."

"No, that's not the quote I was referring to. 'If you're going to seek revenge, dig two graves.' The second one is for yourself. Just be careful, Sam." As he turned the key and opened the door, he nodded at James, who was still keeping watch.

Once inside, Sam momentarily forgot his anger at Judge Ambrose and hopped up onto the seat. *"Something's different. The first time we checked, what was in the ashtray?"*

"Two cigars, one cigarette," I said.

"Right. And now look: no cigarette butt. That's been bugging me since the first time we were in here. It just didn't fit. The salesman is a cigar smoker. Why would there be a cigarette butt in his ashtray?"

"Maybe he had a visitor," said Clarence. "Or maybe the porters forgot to clean the ashtray before we left New York."

"Possibly," said Sam. *"And if the butt were still there, I would probably accept either one of those as reasonable. But there is only one logical explanation for its disappearance: somebody on this train doesn't want us to know that he—or she—was in here."*

Clarence opened the door and asked James to join us inside the compartment. "Has anybody else been inside since I spoke to you?"

"No, sir," said James. "I've been keeping an eye on the door, just like you said."

Clarence thanked him and sent him back into the corridor.

Sam clambered about the room, sniffing and sticking his nose into every corner. *"Mrrr. Did anyone else come in with Judge Ambrose when he made his so-called investigation? How about Reverend Dribble?"*

"Perfiddle," Clarence corrected. "And no, it was just me and the judge, and I was with him the whole time . . . no, wait, I left him alone for a few seconds. There was a noise outside in the corridor, and I went out to make sure nothing was wrong."

"Where was Judge Giganticus when you came back in?" Sam asked.

Clarence closed his eyes for a moment, thinking. "He had his back to me . . . facing the window. And the ashtray. But why—"

"Why would the judge, revered by all—especially his grocer—remove a crucial piece of evidence? Simple. He knows who smoked that cigarette."

I joined Mother and Jessica in the dining car a few minutes later, but I had a hard time focusing on the food in front of me. My eyes darted from table to table and my ears strained to listen to every conversation. In my mind, I kept replaying what Ellie first told me about recognizing the two criminals on board the Shoreliner. Was I forgetting something? If only I'd asked more questions!

"You're awfully quiet tonight," Mother remarked. "Is everything all right? I suppose you're worried about that little girl. When I think about what her poor mother must be going through right now, I could cry."

"She'll be okay . . . I think. I have a feeling."

"I hope you're right. Now, how about your dinner? You seem more interested in what other people are eating and drinking than what's on your own plate. Don't you like it?"

I looked down at my barely touched pork chop, fried potatoes, and applesauce. "No—I mean, yes, it's great." I smiled at her. "I'm just taking my time. I don't want to rush such a nice dinner."

She squeezed my hand across the narrow table. "You're a good boy, Henry. I wish I could give you and your sister fancy dinners like this every night. Things will be better soon—your father says that the ports he visits are starting to get busier. He says it's only a matter of time before the mills in Pittsburgh and Youngstown are back at full strength, and that will mean more cargo for all the G and S ships."

G & S Shipping owned a number of freighters on the Great Lakes, including the *Point Pelee*, captained by Father, but when Mother mentioned the company by name, her face changed suddenly, as if a light had been switched on.

"That little girl," she said, "the one who was kidn—er, the one who is lost—what's her name?"

"Ellie," I said. "Why?"

"Ellie what?"

"Strasbourg."

Mother's hand moved to cover her mouth. "Oh, my."

"What? What's going on?"

"You know that your father works for G and S Shipping, right? *G and S* stands for Gimble and *Strasbourg*. I'm ninety-nine percent certain that Ellie's father is the Strasbourg in Gimble and Strasbourg. I should have caught it when her mother introduced herself. When the newest ship in the fleet was launched a few years back, there was a picture in the newspaper of the christening. The woman who broke the bottle of champagne over the bow was Ellie's mother—Doris Strasbourg—I'm sure of it. And in the picture, she had her daughter with her, who was about your age."

"When she said that her father built ships," I said, "I thought she meant that he *actually* built them, not that he was the guy who . . . owned the company where they got built." I then told her about the newspaper clipping that I had found in the salesman's compartment. "They were going to Conneaut Lake Park for the grand opening of the Blue Streak. She's so lucky; she's going to be on the first ride. Wow, I guess she really was telling the truth about everything."

"What a strange coincidence—all of us being on the same train, you two kids becoming friends."

"I wouldn't exactly call us friends. I only just met her today. Still, it's weird that her dad *owns* the *Point Pelee*. Does Father know him?"

"I don't think so. At least I never heard him mention it. It's a big company, with offices in lots of cities. But you can ask him yourself tomorrow! He should be in port by the time you wake up in the morning."

I smiled at the thought of running down the pier and jumping up to greet him. "I can't wait. It seems like he's been gone forever."

"It's a long way to Duluth and back. At least he'll be home for a few days while they load the *Pelee* for the next trip."

I ducked my head, pretending to be very interested in my food as the woman in dark glasses and her husband started down the aisle of the dining car toward me. As she walked past, her pink cardigan sweater brushed against the table, knocking a fork to the floor. Instinctively, I reached down to pick it up, and found myself nose to nose with the man in the gray suit.

"I've got it," said the man, smiling at me. "Sorry about that. I'll have the waiter send another over. Hey, I remember you. You were looking for that girl, the one who . . . hey, wait up!" He ran down the aisle after his wife, who was already out of sight.

Sam was in his usual position on Clarence's bed, all four feet tucked under his body, eyes closed.

"I can't believe he's sleeping at a time like this!" I said to Clarence, who had motioned to me to join him in the dormitory car a few moments earlier.

"Mrrr. I'm not sleeping, you ninny. I'm thinking."

"Ohhh. Sorry. What were you thinking *about*? Boy, I still can't believe I'm talking to a *cat*."

"It's no picnic for me, either, kid," said Sam. "Out of the two billion people on this planet that I might be able to communicate with—writers, artists, scientists, musicians—I get a train conductor and a ten-, sorry, eleven-year-old kid from Ashtabula, Ohio. Not exactly the cream of the crop. But to answer your question, I was thinking about how nothing in this case makes sense. We're supposed to believe that a traveling salesman kidnaps a rich kid in broad daylight, and then jumps off the train with her stuffed into a sample

case, leaving behind a trail of clues that Hansel and Gretel would be proud of. Just how does an ordinary salesman know that Mrs. Strasbourg will be on this particular train? Or that she'll be carrying this priceless sapphire—the Blue Streak—with her?"

"Well, we know he isn't working alone," said Clarence. "At this moment, somebody must be driving west with Ellie in the car. Maybe he knows someone who works for the Strasbourg family. A maid, a cook, even the kid's nanny. One thing we do know: he really is a salesman. One of the passengers, another traveling salesman from Chicago, remembers him. He's in one of the sections in the same car. Once he described the fellow, I remembered him, too. He's been aboard three or four times in the past couple of years. Spent most of his time in the club car. Nice-looking, six feet tall, with a thick head of black hair, combed straight back, and a Boston Blackie mustache. Real ladies' man."

"Have you run that description by Mrs. Strasbourg?" Sam asked. "It's a long shot, but maybe she'll remember seeing him someplace other than aboard this train."

"That's a great idea, Sam," said Clarence. "I'll do that right away."

Behind me in the dormitory car, someone cleared his throat, and I turned to see a short, rather stout man in a uniform staring at me. He had a strange look on his face as his eyes darted from me to Sam and then to Clarence.

"Oh, sorry, Clarence," he said. "I . . . thought you were just talking to, uh, Sam. Didn't know there was anyone else here."

"That's Oliver, the telegraph operator," said Sam, snickering. "Watch this. The poor guy thinks Clarence is ready for his own tent at Camp Cuckoo. He has this habit of walking in at the wrong moment, and then Clarence has to wriggle his way out of it. At least this time there's another human nearby."

"What? Oh, hi, Oliver. This is Henry Shipley. Just showing him around the train. Do you have something for me?" Clarence asked, pointing at the paper in Oliver's hand.

"Telegram from Albany—the police."

"Oh . . . good. Thank you, Oliver."

Clarence waited for Oliver to leave and then read the telegram aloud so we could hear. "'ARRESTED SALESMAN AT STATE STREET HOTEL STOP SAMPLE CASE FULL OF OLD NEWSPAPERS STOP SALESMAN ANGRY ABOUT MISSING MARBLE SAMPLES STOP NO SIGN OF GIRL STOP'"

"Mrraa. They might as well let him go," said Sam. "Romeo had nothing to do with the kidnapping, but the real kidnappers knew he'd be on this train. They needed a patsy—one with a big, heavy piece of luggage. Something big enough to hold a little girl."

"But—"

"They never actually put her inside. They just wanted us to think

that they did, to throw us off the trail for a while. Who knows what we missed while we were gallivanting around talking about that silly salesman. I can understand you two being fooled, but I should have known better."

Clarence sat on the edge of the bed. "This changes everything. The salesman, the marble samples, the picture—those were our only clues. We don't know *anything*. What do we tell her mother now? And I ought to tell the judge, seeing as he's put himself in charge."

"Don't do anything . . . yet," said Sam. "We're the only ones who know the truth about the salesman, right? Let's just keep it that way . . . for a while."

"I don't get it, Sam," I said. "If that salesman doesn't have Ellie, who does? And if she wasn't in that case, how did they get her off the train without anybody seeing her?"

Sam scratched behind his notched right ear with a back paw. *"Give me a chance to think. Even a brain as powerful as mine needs a little time to work out the details . . . especially when it hasn't been fed in a while."*

Clarence winked at me, grinning at Sam's not-so-subtle hint.

Meanwhile, Sam scratched a little more. *"But this new information makes another conversation that Henry and I overheard more . . . interesting, at least. Did you notice that couple from the* dining car, right before the judge tried to assassinate me? Handsome young fellow in a gray suit, and the dame—hoo boy! She's a real looker, hiding behind dark glasses."

"What was so interesting about them?" Clarence asked. "Besides their looks, that is."

"They *must* be the criminals that Ellie recognized," I said. "The woman said that she was sure that some girl had recognized her. . . . What if she was talking about Ellie? Because then the man said that it was 'too late' for her to say anything. And then he said he was going to 'take care of' some lady in a funny hat, because she recognized them, too. We need to find her, and warn her!"

"Whoa! Keep your knickers on," said Sam. "Sit down. We're not going anywhere, not yet. We need a plan. I need to think—really think. It would help if we knew what room they're in. I think they came from the back part of the train, but it's possible they were just coming from the club car, or the observation lounge. The porters will be able to help us. Maybe if I had something to eat I could think more clearly."

Clarence chuckled. "Oh, are you hungry, Sam? Why didn't you just say so?" He reached under his bed, pulled out a small, flat tin can with a bright red wrapper, and tossed it onto the bed, where it bounced, clunking poor Sam in the head.

"Mrrrraa . . . what are you—" He stopped as the label came into focus: Sail On Sardines. *"I knew it! You were holding out on me, you old son of a gun!"*

A few moments passed, silent except for the sound of Sam licking his lips.

"Ahem. They're not going to open themselves," he finally said.

"Oh, I'm *so* sorry," Clarence said. "Did you want me to open them for you? I would have thought that with a brilliant mind like yours, certainly you could open a simple can of sardines. Beautiful, oily, salty, delicious sardines. And will you look at that—they're your favorite brand. Ohhh, I *forgot*. You don't have one of *these*." Clarence waved a thumb in front of Sam's face.

"Hilarious," said Sam, clearly *not* amused. *"You should consider yourself lucky that I don't have an opposable thumb. That's about the only thing standing between me and world domination."*

"Um, wouldn't it be kind of hard to take over the world when you sleep about twenty hours a day?" I remarked.

"Nice one," said Clarence, winking again.

"All right, all right. You've both had your little fun. Now, about those sardines."

"Oh, right. The sardines. You want them now? I thought maybe you'd want to save them for a . . . special occasion," said Clarence.

"Pish," said Sam. *"If there's one thing I've learned in my eight*

lives, it's that every day is a special occasion. You never know when it's going to be your last. Carpe diem, my friends."

"Car-pay what?" I asked.

"Carpe diem," said Clarence. "It's Latin for 'seize the day.' In other words, take advantage of your opportunities."

"Oh," I said. "About that other thing you said, Sam. I've been meaning to ask you: is it true that cats have nine lives?"

"Of course it's true," said Sam, licking his lips as Clarence rolled back the lid of the can of sardines with the help of the metal key.

I had more questions I wanted to ask about that whole "nine lives" thing, but I became distracted by Clarence opening the can. "Hey, can I have the key?" I asked when he finished. "I collect them." They ate a lot of sardines and anchovies on the *Point Pelee,* and the cook started saving them for me when I was only seven. Back home in Ashtabula, I had two quart jars full of them.

"You collect sardine can keys?" Sam asked, incredulous. *"What on earth for?"*

"Nothing special. I just like them." Clarence threw me the key.

When I was sticking the key into my pants pocket, something sharp stabbed my hand—the barrette! I had completely forgotten about it! I took it out of my pocket and polished the engraved oval surface on my pants until it glistened like a mirror.

"What have you got there?" Clarence asked.

I set the barrette on the bed, next to the sardine can. "I found this on the floor, right after the train stopped in Albany."

"Hmmm. Nice," said Sam. *"Looks like sterling silver, good quality. What, exactly, is it?"*

"It's called a barrette," I said. "Girls use them to . . . they put them in their hair."

"Does this barrette have some special significance, or are you interrupting my dinner out of spite?" Sam asked.

"Knock, knock," said a voice out in the vestibule. "Mr. Nockwood?"

"Come in," said Clarence. "Ah, Reverend Perfiddle. What can I do for you?"

"I was wondering if I could talk to you for a moment—in private."

Clarence disappeared into the vestibule to talk to him, leaving me to finish telling the story of the barrette to Sam alone.

"I don't *know* that it is important, but there's something funny—funny strange, that is—about it. Like I said, it was right after the Albany stop, right after I was talking to you. I was heading toward the back of the train, looking for Ellie, when I got stuck behind a family that had just boarded. There were three of them. The dad, who was carrying a girl with long red hair—she was sleeping, with her face against his shoulder, so I couldn't tell how old she was— and the mom, whose hair was exactly the same color. They were right in front of me, and all of a sudden, *this* drops onto the floor and bounces under a seat. I was *sure* it came from one of them, but when I tried to give it to the lady, she said it wasn't hers or her daughter's. There was nobody else around, so I don't know where else it could have come from."

Sam yawned. *"Kid, you're killing me. Where are you going with this story? So some dame dropped a barrette and didn't want it back. Big deal. Now, why don't you tell me more about this little hobby of yours. How many cans of sardines would you say the cook aboard your pop's ship has stocked away? A couple hundred? More?"*

"Boy, you really do have a one-track mind," I said. "I'm not done with my story yet. What I was trying to say is, don't you think it's a little fishy that she wouldn't want something so nice back?"

"Sorry, kid, but I have to interrupt you again. I'm not really comfortable with people using the word fishy as a synonym for suspicious," said Sam. *"Fishy should always be considered a good thing. But go on."*

"You see, I kept my eyes open all through dinner, watching everybody who came into the dining car, and I never saw them—the man, the woman, the kid. None of them had dinner. They'd be kind of hard to miss with all that red hair."

Another yawn from Sam, this one louder and longer. *"One more time: so? Maybe they brought their own sandwiches. Maybe they forgot about dinner. Maybe they got off the train at Schenectady—"*

"We didn't stop at Schenectady."

"Oh, right. I knew that."

"You could be right about the sandwiches; my mom does that sometimes. I just think it's . . . strange, that's all. Okay, okay, I'll stop talking about it. For now."

"Good. Now, let's go spy on Clarence and Reverend Perfiddle, and see what that little visit was all about."

Don't Call Me Samantha
THE ALMOST ENTIRELY TRUE
AUTOBIOGRAPHY OF LANTERN SAM

What Goes Up . . .

I'm not proud of the humiliating conclusion to this chapter of my life, but I swore to tell the unvarnished truth, so here it is: bruised and bloodied, but with a belly full of roast chicken, I slept for fourteen hours straight on Walt's boat. (After the *Susie G* incident, I had sworn off boats for life, but I think we can all agree that after surviving Tom the Tomcat, a demented rooster, and the Cleveland sewer system, I was entitled to a night in a warm, dry cabin.)

Don't get me wrong. I appreciated all that Walt had done for me, but I just wasn't ready for a long-term commitment—especially with someone who lived on a boat—so I quietly limped away from the dock when he went off to buy groceries for the next leg of his voyage. Even though the odds of running into Marmalade and Tom were slim, I was taking no chances, so I headed due south, away from the city and away from the water. After traveling two days on paw, I caught a ride on a southbound freight train. As we passed by one dairy farm after another, I started craving fresh milk so badly that I jumped off at the first opportunity, a small town called Hiram.

It didn't take me long to find what I was looking for; the scent of Jersey cows was like perfume to me, and I simply followed my nose until I found myself in a pasture with a whole herd. At milking time, I tagged along and then slipped into the barn unnoticed. My heart leapt when the first cat I saw was another calico. It meant that I would have a place to rest, and all the fresh milk I could drink. You see, calicoes are not like other cats; we live and die by a sacred code.

Another calico must always be treated like family, Mom told my siblings and me. *No matter the circumstances.*

That's when Mom recited "The Rhyme of the Ancient Calico," a poem about a silent, broken-down cat who was turned away from barn after barn on a snowy January night. The next day, he was found dead in a snowdrift, where an older cat recognized him as Jedediah, a member of the Calicium, also known as the Council of Calicoes. The Calicium was made up of three elder calicoes, one for each of our colors. For many centuries, they met once a year under a half-moon and recited verses in the old language. With the death of Jedediah, however, a third of the secret was lost forever, as he had never passed his knowledge on to another. At first no one noticed anything different, but slowly the truth became clear. From every corner of the world, the news was the same, litter after litter, year after year: no male calicoes were born.

And nothing can change that, calicoes believe, until the lost verses are rediscovered. In the meantime, we live by the Calico Code and treat all strangers like family, reciting verses from the epic poem "The Rhyme of the Ancient Calico" whenever we meet.

I tiptoed across the floor of the barn and slowly approached the other calico. I touched my left front paw to my forehead and chest, and then spoke the opening lines of the sacred poem:

"From lands unknown the gentle stranger hailed,
Seeking shelter from winter's frigid breath."

The other calico continued without missing a beat:

"But at every door, love and kindness failed,
And on he wandered, to a lonely death."

Then, as the code requires, we touched noses and introduced ourselves.

"Sam, Linesville, Pennsylvania."

"Billie, Hiram, Ohio. Welcome to Twin Elms Farm, Sam. Sorry if I'm staring. You're my first male calico. And if you don't mind my saying, you look like somebody's been using you for a scratching post."

"Tough night in the city," I said.

"Well, feel free to stay as long as you like. At the moment, there's just me and Ginny—that's her over by those calves—so there's plenty of milk. Ginny's deaf and mostly blind, so she probably won't even notice you're here."

"Anything I need to worry about? Roosters, for instance?"

"No, nothing like that. Well, no, that's not quite true. Can't forget about Daisy."

"Daisy?"

"A Chihuahua."

"What's that, some kind of chicken?"

Billie laughed. "It's a kind of dog," she said.

"Ohhh. Big?"

"No, only about half my size." She shook her head, reconsidering. "Actually, she's not quite that big."

I had never heard of such a thing. "Are you *sure* it's a dog?"

"Oh, she's a dog, all right. An unholy terror. Just keep an eye out for her; she's sneaky. And *fast*."

I couldn't tell if she was pulling my leg. A tiny, dangerous dog? Didn't seem possible.

My first few days with Billie at Twin Elms Farm were a slice of homemade sardine pie. My wounds began to heal (although my right ear was permanently notched, thanks to Tom's wicked left hook), my stomach was always full, and the straw in the loft was softer and sweeter smelling than any I had ever slept on. Each day the weather turned a little colder, and I made up my mind to take up Billie's offer to spend the winter in the comfort of the dairy barn.

October turned into November, and I still hadn't seen Daisy. I kidded Billie about it one evening, chiding her for making up such a crazy story.

She laughed. "Just you wait, Sam. Daisy is all too real. She is not to be trifled with."

The very next day, Billie and I were in a small pasture next to the house stalking field mice when out of the corner of my eye, I saw something running toward us. For a moment, I was confused.

"Look at the size of that rat," I said.

"That's no rat," said Billie. "It's Daisy! Run for your life!" She ducked under the barbed wire and bolted for the barn.

But I stood my ground. I wasn't about to be bullied by a dog less than half my size. Clearly it was time for somebody to teach Daisy a lesson, so I puffed myself up and extended my sharpest claws. Only a fool would dare to get within swinging range.

When she was about twenty feet away and closing fast, I realized that I had made a horrible, and possibly fatal, mistake. I still have nightmares about the look in that crazy mutt's eyes as she barreled straight into me, snarling and snapping those razor-like teeth. I spat and hissed and scratched with everything I had, but I don't think she even noticed! I had only one option left: retreat. I turned and ran faster than I had ever run, with Daisy nipping at my heels all the way across the yard as the farmer and his wife, who had just left the barn, stared openmouthed.

I swore to myself when I realized that they had closed the barn door, and then swerved out toward the front yard, where a pair of stately old elm trees stood. I hit the closer of the two at full speed with all seventeen claws extended for climbing. A split second later, Daisy ran into the tree so hard that she knocked herself out cold for about ten seconds. Meanwhile, I kept on climbing, not stopping until I found myself a comfy spot on a branch about fifty feet above the ground.

By then Daisy was awake and absolutely furious that I

had somehow escaped her jaws of death. She bounced up and down, looking as if she were on a trampoline, and then changed tactics, trying to climb the elm tree, again and again. She would make it a few feet up—far enough to concern me, at least the first few times—and then fall backward, yelping at me as if it were all *my* fault.

That went on for more than an hour. The farmer's wife brought out a leash, but dear old Daisy refused to let anyone get close enough to put it on. She snarled at her owners and ran faster and faster around the base of the tree until they gave up trying. I'm sure they were thinking what I was thinking: sooner or later, the stupid dog would give up.

Of course, even if she did finally admit defeat, I was still left with one big problem. I knew how to climb *up*. Getting down? That was another story. I had a vague memory of something my mother had said about going backward, but the details were hazy. (In general, she told us never to climb higher than we were willing to jump down from, but it was too late for *that* piece of advice to be useful to me.) With Daisy showing no signs of slowing, I figured that I would cross that bridge when I came to it. Snuggled into the notch between my branch and the tree trunk, and prepared to wait as long as necessary, I closed my eyes to think for a while.

Billie, thank goodness, was the only witness to what happened next.

In short, I fell out of the tree. One second I was safe and secure, and the next I was, according to Billie, "dropping like an apple that's been shaken from its branch."

About halfway down, I sensed that something was wrong and opened my eyes, realizing too late that I was plummeting toward Daisy, with nothing between us except air. Lucky for me, she was sound asleep, exhausted from hours of barking and running in circles, and she never saw me coming.

I tried to miss her, but it was no use. Gravity won the battle, and I landed belly-first with a screeching thud on poor Daisy's back, then bounced into the grass next to her.

The fall alone should have killed me, and I still can't explain how Daisy survived the collision, either. A high school physics student could tell us that when ten pounds of cat drops from fifty feet and hits three pounds of Chihuahua, well, it isn't pretty. I've always preferred to think of it the way pilots talk about airplane landings: if you can walk away from it, it was a good one.

In this case, Daisy and I both walked away—but not immediately. The crash knocked the wind out of both of us, and according to Billie, neither of us moved a muscle for a good ten seconds. Finally, I raised my head and made eye contact with Daisy as we lifted ourselves to our paws, testing all of our limbs to make sure they were still attached and working. Then I began to back away, still not taking my eyes off Daisy, afraid to make any sudden movements. She stood in place, her head cocked to one side, watching my every move.

At the moment I was about to turn and race toward the barn, something miraculous happened: Daisy wagged her tail at me! And not in an I-can't-wait-to-tear-you-apart way, either. It was the genuine article, a left-left-left wag (which every cat learns to recognize as the friendliest kind), and I froze in my tracks, mesmerized.

I turned to Billie, who had left the safety of the barn to watch. "Are you seeing what I'm seeing?" I asked. "Has she ever done this before?"

"Never," said Billie. "She must be dreaming. You'd better get out of there before she wakes up."

As if she sensed our wariness, Daisy flopped over onto her back, rolling around in the grass—in other words, acting like a completely normal, silly dog. Then she leaped to her feet and ran around the tree four or five times before nudging me playfully with her nose.

"I think she wants you to chase her," said Billie. "Well, this is a story I'll tell my grandchildren: the day Sam fell asleep in a tree, dropped fifty feet, and knocked the mean right out of a Chihuahua."

"I wasn't sleeping," I said. "I was resting my eyes. *Thinking*."

Chapter 6

Near the back of the train, two cars in front of the observation car, Clarence held open the door to drawing room B as Reverend Perfiddle helped his pregnant wife through the narrow entrance. Sam and I hid at the bend in the corridor where the wider drawing rooms started.

"Lucky for you, we have this one empty drawing room," said Clarence. "I think she'll be much more comfortable in here. Do you think she's going into labor?"

Reverend Perfiddle guided his wife to the bed and helped ease her down on it. "How are you feeling, my dear? Do you think it's . . . time?"

Mrs. Perfiddle took several deep breaths through her mouth before attempting to speak. "No . . . not yet . . . oh!"

"What is it?"

"Just a little twinge. There, it's gone," she said.

"Shall I ask around for a doctor?" Clarence said. "There's bound to be one aboard."

"No, not yet," said Mrs. Perfiddle. "It's not time. A woman knows these things. Thank you, Mr. . . . Nockwood. You've been most kind. I just need to rest for a while."

Reverend Perfiddle grasped Clarence's hand with both of his own and hurried him out the door. "Thank you, thank you, and God bless you. Right now, I think she needs peace and quiet, and rest. We shouldn't disturb her further, I think."

"You'll let me know if you need anything?" said Clarence as the door closed in his face.

"Ellie Strasbourg is still on the Shoreliner," announced Sam as Clarence joined us in the corridor.

"What?" I shouted. "How do you know?"

"Oh, I've known that for a while," he said. *"It's simple deduction. Clearly she didn't get off the train. Therefore she's still on the train."*

"Then come on," I said. "If she's on the train, why can't we just search every room until we find her?"

"Even if Sam is right—which, I have to admit, he usually is—it's not quite that easy," said Clarence. "First, there are ninety-six rooms on this train. People pay good money for those rooms, and they expect to be left alone to sleep or relax or play cards or whatever it is they want to do. There are pregnant women, and children, and elderly passengers aboard—I have a responsibility to them."

"What about Ellie?" I asked. "Don't you have a responsibility to her? And her mom?"

Clarence sighed. "I hear you, Henry, and I know how you feel. But the fact is, even if I wanted to, I don't have the authority to do it—only the police can do things like that, and even they can't search a room unless they have a reason—and a search warrant."

"What about Judge Ambrose? Can he do it?"

Clarence shook his head. "He's a *retired* sheriff, not a cop or a G-man. Even the fact that he's a judge doesn't help, either."

"I'm afraid he's right," said Sam. *"But that doesn't mean we're done looking for Ellie—not by a long shot. My brain is just getting warmed up."*

"You see?" said Clarence. "We still have some time before the train gets to Dunkirk and Mrs. Strasbourg has to hand over that necklace, but we have to put our brains together. Now, what were you saying about that barrette when we were interrupted?"

I filled in the missing details for him while he listened, nodding.

"There's only one problem with your story," said Clarence, rubbing his chin thoughtfully. "No passengers boarded at Albany."

"Are you sure? I was right behind them. They looked like they just got on board."

"Where exactly did you see them?"

"One car behind the dormitory car. I first saw them coming out of the space between the cars, the, um . . ."

"Vestibule," said Clarence. "Did they have luggage?"

I closed my eyes and re-created the scene in my mind. "I don't . . . no. The man was carrying the girl, that's all."

"So you didn't actually see them board the train," noted Lantern Sam in his cross-examination.

"No . . . but . . . they were . . ." I was getting flustered as I realized that I couldn't state for certain that they had boarded the train in Albany.

"Let me see that barrette again," said Sam.

"What are you thinking, Sam?" Clarence asked, looking over my shoulder as I held the barrette up for Sam to see.

"More light," Sam demanded. *"Over here . . . stop! Well, well, well. Take another look, boys. I really am getting sloppy; should have seen this before. It's the engraving. At first, I thought it was just decoration, a floral pattern of some kind. But it's more than that. It's initials, a monogram. A big script S surrounded by E and*

M. *The engraving is so light, and the initials all overlap, making it hard to read."*

"The S would be the last name. That's the way monograms usually work. Must be *E.M.S.*," said Clarence.

"It's Ellie's!" I cried. "It has to be. I'll bet you anything that her middle initial is *M*. Ellie M. Strasbourg."

"That's easy enough to find out," said Clarence. "If this is Ellie's, her mother will certainly recognize it. Let's go talk to her."

"Wait, does this mean that . . . um, what does this mean?" I asked, one step behind the conductor.

"How sure are you that this barrette came from either the woman or the little girl with red hair?" Sam asked. *"Give me a number. Ten percent? Fifty? Seventy-five?"*

I considered the question for a few seconds, replaying the incident in my mind. "Ninety-nine percent. Either that or it fell from the sky."

"Then I'd say there's a one percent chance that the girl being carried was not Ellie."

"B-but she had—"

"Red hair, I know. Easy. A wig. Probably two—one for the mother, too, to make it seem really obvious that they were mother and daughter."

"They were already on the train," said Clarence, "just waiting for their chance. When they saw her alone, they pounced. Bet they followed her to the end of the train and got her with the chloroform. Probably in one of the lavatories. All they had to do was throw a wig and a coat on her and carry her back to their room. They could have walked right past Ellie's mother and she wouldn't have known. Then they ditch the wigs and—ta-da!—they blend in with everybody else."

To the back of the train we hurried, with Sam padding along at our feet, until we reached the observation car. Standing and talking outside the Commodore Perry suite were the handsome young porter, James, and the Strasbourgs' beautiful maid, Julia. James snapped to attention when he saw Clarence.

"Mr. Nockwood, sir. I was . . . making sure . . ."

"I asked James to bring a sandwich from the kitchen . . . for Mrs. Strasbourg," said Julia. "I tried to get her to eat something, but she's too worried. Have you heard anything?"

"That's why we're here," said Clarence. "We have some . . . is Mrs. Strasbourg alone?"

"Yes, sir." Julia went inside and closed the door, reopening it a few seconds later. "Come inside."

Mrs. Strasbourg, violently wringing her hands together, her face stained from tears, moved toward Clarence. "You have news about Ellie, Mr. Nockwood?"

"Yes, ma'am. There have been some developments. You should sit."

Expecting the worst, she cried out, "Oh . . . oh, no," but stopped when Clarence waved his hand back and forth.

"It's not bad news, ma'am. It may even be good news." He held out the barrette. "Do you recognize this?"

She burst into tears as she took the barrette. "It's Ellie's! I gave it to her for her birthday last year. Where did you find it?"

Clarence pointed at me. "Henry found it in the corridor of the train. There was a man carrying a child, and we think . . ." He had to stop because Mrs. Strasbourg was sobbing so loudly.

Finally, she composed herself, and she listened as Clarence told her the truth about the salesman and Sam's theory of how the kidnapping occurred.

"I'm not sure I understand," she said. "You think . . ."

"We're *certain* that she's still on the train," said Clarence.

"Still on the train," repeated Mrs. Strasbourg, collapsing into one of the wing chairs. "Just knowing that makes me feel so much better. The thought of my baby girl locked in that box, being carted around like a piece of luggage—" When she burst into tears again, Julia knelt beside her, comforting her.

"We have an advantage at the moment," said Clarence. "The kidnappers don't know that *we* know that Ellie is still on the train. I know every inch of the Shoreliner, and you have to trust me, ma'am. No one is getting off until Ellie is safe and sound. You have my promise. If they think we're chasing after a marble salesman and a large trunk, they're going to let their guard down sooner or later. And when they do, we're going to catch them. I'll be back shortly. In the meantime, don't leave this room, and whatever you do, *don't* let that necklace out of your sight."

The door to the Commodore Perry suite closed behind us, and our eyes landed on Judge Ambrose and Reverend Perfiddle in the observation car lounge, in the midst of a serious-looking conversation. Smoke from the minister's cigarette formed a wispy gray cloud around his head, while the judge champed at yet another unlit cigar, like an old cow working her cud.

"Mr. Nockwood," said Ambrose through gritted teeth. "I see you still have your friends with you." He nodded toward Sam and me.

The fur on Sam's back stood straight up, and he began to growl, a deep, frightening sound that made me take a step backward.

"Come on, Sam. Let's get out of here," I said, heading for

the front of the car, where Sam joined me. To Clarence, I added, "We'll meet you up in the dormitory."

I made lots of noise as I pretended to stomp out of the car, heading toward the front of the train, but that's all it was: pretending. There was a small storage area near the front of the car, and Sam and I ducked into it so we could hear what was being said.

Clarence took a deep breath before addressing the two men. "Mr. Ambrose. Reverend Perfiddle. Is your wife resting comfortably?"

"Yes, yes she is," said the reverend, raising his drink to Clarence. "Thank you for your assistance."

Judge Ambrose snapped at Clarence, "Why were you in Mrs. Strasbourg's room? I hope it was nothing to do with her daughter. Haven't I made it clear that I'm in charge of that situation?"

"My, my," said Sam. "The judge certainly is jumpy. Why is he so worried that Clarence might be talking to Mrs. Strasbourg? What does he think is going to happen?"

"Absolutely clear, Mr. Ambrose," said Clarence. "Her maid had asked a porter to bring some food back, and I was merely checking to ensure that she was in need of nothing further."

"I see. Have you anything else to report? Any news about our salesman friend?"

"No," Clarence lied, probably a bit too quickly. "How about you? Anything you'd care to share? I take it that you have completed your investigation?"

"Humph," said Ambrose. "Yes, I have. My conclusions haven't changed one bit. I still believe exactly what I believed five minutes after this case landed in my lap: a criminal, pretending to be a traveling salesman working by himself, abducted that little girl and carried her off the train with the help of an emptied-out sample case . . . and a conductor and porters too blind—or lazy—to see what was right under their noses. You see, Mr. Nockwood, these criminal types aren't as clever, or industrious, as the newspapers would have you believe. In my experience, the average criminal is both stupid and lazy."

"Well, I suppose that when it comes to criminals, you're the expert," said Clarence.

"Nice one, Clarence," said Sam. *"It went right over his head."*

Reverend Perfiddle snubbed out his cigarette in the ashtray and then raised his eyebrows at Clarence. "I believe that Judge Ambrose has done all that can be done . . . under the circumstances. We owe him—and dear Mrs. Strasbourg, of course—our loyalty and, perhaps, our prayers. Mrs. Strasbourg has received her instructions regarding this Blue Streak necklace; our job is to support her, to help her in any way we can."

"*Smooth, Reverend Piddlepot, very smooth,*" murmured Sam. "*What is your angle?*"

"What do you mean?" I whispered.

"*I mean, why is he in such a hurry to help out Judge Hambone? They're awful cozy—I wonder if they knew each other before this trip.*"

"Maybe the judge goes to Reverend Perfiddle's church," I suggested.

Sam scoffed. "*Ha! Pardon me for not believing that the judge is a regular churchgoer. Unless they have a buffet table set up in the back of the church.*"

"Hey, that *would* be pretty nice. If the minister was really boring, you could go back and make yourself a sandwich."

"*Would there be sardines in this buffet?*"

"Boy, you *really* like sardines, don't you? Okay, fine, we'll have sardines."

Luckily, that silly conversation was cut short when a woman got up from her seat in the very back of the observation section—the same seat I'd been in when Ellie first spied on me—and started making her way toward us.

"Good evening, gentlemen," she said as she passed Clarence, Judge Ambrose, and Reverend Perfiddle.

Clarence tipped his cap at her, and all three men chanted, "Evening, ma'am."

And then I saw it: the hat to end all hats! A pair of realistic-looking goldfinches perched on twigs that wrapped around a yellow brim, which was so bright it glowed. It was the wackiest, *yellowest* hat I'd ever seen. She just had to be the lady that the guy in the gray suit was talking about, because there's no way there were *two* hats like that in the whole world.

Sam couldn't take his eyes off it, either. *"What the—? Are those real birds?"* he asked, licking his lips as she walked by. Maybe there *was* something he liked as much as sardines, after all.

"Let's follow her," I said. "I want to ask her something."

"Mrrraaa. So do I."

"No, Sam, you can't have her birds. Besides, I doubt if they're real."

"We'd better get a closer look . . . just to be sure."

We followed the hat, stalking our prey like a hunter and his trusty hound—except I didn't have a shotgun over my shoulder, and Lantern Sam was a cat. When we got to the dining car, it had been transformed into a miniature nightclub (or a miniature version of ones I'd seen in the movies, anyway). The lights were dimmed and every table was filled with people listening to the music of Gladys and Gwendolyn Henshaw—the sisters who had spoken to the marble salesman. They sat side by side on the piano bench,

Gladys's fingers racing over the keys while Gwendolyn sang "Rock and Roll," a song made famous by the Boswell Sisters. What I didn't know about music was a lot, but they sounded pretty good to me.

Sam was not quite as impressed. *"Ouch. Make them stop. They're hurting my ears. They're worse than Clarence in the bathtub. Believe me, you do not want to hear that."*

"Shhh!" I said, forgetting for a second that I was the only one who could hear Sam. In front of me, a man who was in the middle of whispering something in his wife's ear thought I was talking to him. He turned and shot me a dirty look.

"Nice going, kid," said Sam. *"Pick a fight with the meanest-looking guy here."*

"Shut up!"

"Do you have a problem, kid?" the man asked, his eyes boring into my head.

"What? No, I'm sorry. I didn't mean—"

Sam chuckled to himself as I retreated to a safe spot on the other side of the room, next to the lady in the bird hat. She was singing along with Gladys and Gwendolyn, and she smiled at me as I elbowed my way into the narrow space between her and the window.

The song ended and everyone clapped loudly. "They're

so good," she said. "They sound just like the Boswell Sisters!"

"*So, let's get this straight: she wears dead birds on her head and she's tone-deaf,*" sniped Sam. "*Gee, do you suppose there are any more at home like her?*"

I gave him the stink eye; I had learned my lesson about shushing him the usual way.

"I know! I thought they were the Boswell Sisters," I said, pretending to be starstruck. "Do you think they're famous?"

Crazy-hat lady shook her head, and the two goldfinches bobbed back and forth. "Oh, I don't think so, but you never know, do you? Last week on the train from Chicago, who do you think sat down to breakfast right across from me? Mr. Gary Cooper, that's who. He was *so* handsome. Even more than he is in the pictures."

"Do you think there's anybody famous on *this* train?" I asked, as wide-eyed and innocent-looking as I could make myself.

She bent down and tried to look me in the eyes, but I couldn't take mine off those stupid goldfinches!

"Can you keep a secret?" she whispered.

"Uh-huh."

"I don't want to mention any names, because everyone

knows they're not married and it's absolutely *scandalous* that they are sharing a compartment, but there is a certain famous couple in drawing room B-3. After the outrage they committed last week, it's no wonder that they're in hiding! Everyone is after them!"

"Really? Room B-3, you say?"

She nodded, then put her index finger to her lips as Gladys and Gwendolyn broke into "The Object of My Affection," another big hit for the Boswell Sisters.

I motioned to Sam, who was sniffing around the entrance to the kitchen, to follow me into the sleeper right behind the dining car.

"That woman with the sunglasses was right!" I exclaimed. "The crazy-hat lady *did* recognize her! And not only that, she knows what compartment they're in—B-3! What should we do? Ellie could be in there right now!"

"Slow down, kid. Take a breath. That's better. B-3, you say? Let's have a look."

"Just like that? Shouldn't we . . . talk about it or something?"

"What is there to talk about? C'mon! Shake a leg, kid." He trotted down the corridor in the direction of the drawing room.

"Wait up! What am I supposed to do—just knock on the door?"

"Works for me."

"What if somebody answers?"

"That's easy. Just play dumb. That shouldn't be too hard for you."

"Heyyy!"

"Oh, relax, kid. I'm just pulling your tail . . . a little. Look, these compartments are small. When they open the door, poke your nose right in there and see what you can see."

"And then what?" I asked. As I traced my finger over the brass *B-3* on the door, my pulse quickened.

"Apologize. Tell them you must have the wrong room, that you were looking for your friend . . . Bobby, or Teddy. And then run like the dickens. You can do it, kid."

I pinched myself on the arm to make sure I wasn't dreaming. "Great. I'm taking advice from a cat."

"You could do worse. Knock, knock."

"Okay, okay." I took a breath, then rapped softly on the door and pressed my ear to it. "I don't hear anything." I knocked again, louder. Still nothing. "Now what?"

A porter I hadn't seen before came toward me, his arms full of blankets.

"Quick—ask him to let you in," said Sam. *"Tell him you forgot your key."* Sensing my hesitation at telling such a blatant lie, he added, *"We don't have much time, kid. If Ellie's in there, we need to help her."*

The porter stopped a few feet in front of me, smiling broadly. "Did you forget your key, young man?"

"Um, yes, yes, that's it. My mother's back in the club car listening to the music . . . she's making me go to bed."

"Here, let me help you," he said, taking out his passkey. He unlocked the door and opened it just a crack for me.

"Thanks. Thanks a lot," I said.

The porter nodded and left us.

"The coast is clear," said Sam. *"Inside, quick!"*

I pushed the door open the rest of the way, hit the light switch, and stepped inside with Sam one step behind me.

Staring up at me from the floor, her eyes squinting at the bright light, was Ellie, gagged and handcuffed to the steel handrail next to the seat.

"Holy macaroni! Ellie! Are you okay?" I asked.

"'Elp 'e! 'Et 'e out of 'ere!" she tried to shout, but the cotton handkerchief absorbed all but the tiniest bit of the sound.

"What do I do, what do I do?" I asked Sam. "She's handcuffed. We have to get Clarence."

"'On't 'eave 'e!" cried Ellie.

"We'll be right back," I said.

Ellie's eyes looked as if they would pop out of her head. "'Atch out!"

And then the lights went out.

Don't Call Me Samantha

THE ALMOST ENTIRELY TRUE AUTOBIOGRAPHY OF LANTERN SAM

Saved by Sardines

I stayed on with Billie at Twin Elms Farm through the long winter, but as the last of the snow melted, those old feelings of wanderlust sprouted along with the first spring crocuses and daffodils. Meanwhile, news about Daisy's sudden transformation spread through the area, and other cats began to show interest in the barn at Twin Elms. When an old friend of Billie's—a dapper tuxedo named Alistair—appeared late one night, I knew that the time had come for me to move on.

Daisy escorted me to the stream that marked the boundary of the farm and showed me where I could cross without getting my paws wet. For a few seconds, we stared at each other from opposite sides of the stream; we then barked and meowed our goodbyes, and I struck out on a path heading east. Ten minutes later, I reached the top of a ridge overlooking Twin Elms Farm and saw that Daisy hadn't moved from her spot—she was still watching me.

It had been nearly eight months since I'd left the Dillys, and I was a little homesick. I had heard snippets of news about my siblings through the cat channels (the cat-news grapevine) but I was eager to see them all, so I began to work my way east toward the Pennsylvania border.

Well, that was my plan, anyway.

Two days after saying goodbye to Billie and Daisy, I stepped onto a train platform from a boxcar that I had shared with a stinky-but-friendly hobo named Franklin. The town was Andover, Ohio, just across the border from my hometown of Linesville. There was no train between the two towns, but I figured that I could make it the rest of the way on paw once I'd rustled up a little something to eat and a comfortable spot to sleep for the night. I turned west toward the town square as a warm spring breeze rattled my whiskers, stirring happy memories in my gut.

Who knows what direction my life might have taken if I hadn't caught a whiff of the intoxicating aroma of sardines at that very moment. Or if I hadn't been hungry, and simply ignored it. But I did and I was, so I had no choice but to investigate further. Cats are, as everyone knows, naturally curious, and if we have one fault, it is that we often let our curiosity get the best of us. This may have been one of those times—I'll let you decide.

I lifted my nose, which has never let me down, high in the air and inhaled deeply. There was no doubt about it. Somewhere close by—*very* close by—there were sardines, and plenty of them. I followed the trail to the back of a seedy joint called Norm's Diner, on the corner of the square. A screen door, patched in several spots, was the only thing between me and the pot of gold at the end of a fishy-smelling rainbow. At first, I thought I was dreaming, or that my tired eyes were playing tricks on me, but nope, it was the real thing, bigger than life—a football-sized can of Sail On brand sardines. It was the most beautiful thing I'd ever seen.

I wiped away a tear and composed myself in the alley behind the diner. Lined up against a wooden fence at the back of the lot was a row of metal trash bins. And if there are sardines inside the restaurant, then those trash bins must be chock-full of empty sardine cans, right? And a little bit of Sail On sardine oil is better than nothing. In fact, it's better than anything—except whole sardines *and* their oil.

The lids were on the trash cans, but that only slowed me down for a moment. Right before I met Marmalade, I'd watched a cat jump onto a lid in order to get the can moving, and then ride it back and forth until it tipped over. Pure genius. So I took a running leap at the first can in the row, landing on the lid. It must have been top-heavy, because when it went down, it started a chain reaction that took the other four cans with it. And *that,* as you might imagine, made a tremendous racket. It brought the cook flying out of the kitchen, waving a giant cleaver, so I scurried into a dark corner away from the action.

"Ach! Doggone those raccoons! I gonna keel you, you good-for-nothings!" he shouted into the darkness before ducking back inside and slamming the door.

"What was that all about?" whispered a female voice mere inches from me.

I jumped straight up, completely caught off guard.

"Sheesh! I just lost a whole life," I said when I could breathe again. "How long have you been there?"

"A few minutes," she said, stepping out into the light.

She was no Marmalade, but she wasn't half bad. And in my own defense, it was no wonder that she'd been able to sneak up on me like that. Coal black from nose to tail, she was a walking, talking, cat-shaped shadow. I wasn't surprised, then, when she introduced herself.

"I'm Shadow. Sorry to scare you like that. Happens all the time."

"I can see why," I said. "I'm Sam. I grew up over in Linesville. Let me guess: you have an all-white brother named Light, don't you?"

She laughed. "No, but I have a sister named Shade. She's gray, not quite as dark as I am. So, Sam from Linesville, what are you looking for?"

"Oh, I don't know. I suppose I'd like to find a little place in the country, with fresh air and good milk, and someone nice to settle down with—you know, the usual things."

Shadow laughed again, a bit louder. "No—I mean, what are you looking for *right now*, in the trash?"

Lucky for me, cats don't blush. "Ohhh. Of course. The *trash*. I was, uh, looking for, uh . . ." She had me so befuddled that I had forgotten what treasure I had so desperately been seeking just moments earlier. Suddenly it all came back to me: "Sardines!"

"What's that?" asked Shadow.

"You've never had sardines? They're fish. They come in a can. They're delicious."

"Like tuna?"

"Hmm. Yes and no. They're both fish in a can, but there's really no comparison. Look, I *like* tuna." I dug through the spilled trash until I found what I was looking for and then pushed a can with the familiar Sail On label toward Shadow. "But for these? For these I'm willing to go to war."

"I see," she said, purring. "You're a very passionate cat, aren't you, Sam from Linesville?"

"I just know what I like." I licked the inside of the can and then motioned to Shadow to do the same. "Come on, give it a try."

She moved next to me and used her tongue to get the last few drops of precious sardine oil. "Oh my. That *is* good."

"And that's not even the best part. Look, there's an open can that's bigger than me inside. You wait here. I'm going in after those delectable fish."

"Are you sure? That cook seems kind of crazy."

"No problem. I'll be in and out so fast he won't even notice."

Even as I said the words, I knew I was tempting fate, but it was too late to take them back.

Crouching next to the screen door, I waited until the cook left the kitchen and the kid washing dishes had his back to me. Using my sharpest claw, I sliced an opening in a weak spot that had already been patched once, and then slipped inside. In one motion, I was on the counter and scooping out sardines as fast as I could. They hung from both sides of my mouth, making me look as if I had a huge, droopy mustache. When I could fit no more, I escaped the kitchen and sprinted back to the dark corner where Shadow sat waiting silently.

I placed the booty—half a dozen lovely little fish—in the Sail On can and stepped back. "Ladies first."

For a cat who had never tasted sardines before, Shadow wasted no time in polishing off all six. "Oh," she said, licking her lips when she finished. "I should have saved you some. Those were delicious."

"Don't worry; there's more," I said, pointing at the screen door. "Back in a flash."

I dashed through the opening in the screen, popped up onto the counter, and stuck my nose into the can. Temptation got to me, however. Sure, Shadow was cute, but I couldn't risk her eating everything I set in front of her—again. So I dug into those beauties like there was no tomorrow, gulping down half a dozen in mere seconds. I had just lifted sardine number seven when the door between the kitchen and the dining room swung open and the cook spotted me.

I stared back at him, my mouth dripping with sardines, my eyes big as salad plates.

"Hey!" he bellowed, running after me.

In my hurry to go, I kicked the rest of that giant can of sardines onto the floor, where it landed upside down with a splash. Meanwhile, the dishwasher, who was terrified of cats for some strange religious reason, ran screaming from the kitchen, knocking the screen door completely off its hinges.

Then, of course, he crossed paths with Shadow, which sent him over the fence and into the town square, still bawling like a baby.

What happened next I know only because Shadow witnessed the whole thing.

The cook chased after me, grabbing his favorite cleaver along the way. Like a circus knife thrower, he wound up, aimed it at me, and let it fly.

I was saved from certain decapitation by a strange twist of fate, which is further proof that sardines are all-powerful: At the exact moment the cook let go of the cleaver, he stepped in the spilled sardine oil and his feet slid out from under him. Into the air he flew, his substantial backside landing with a splat in a mountain of sardines. Meanwhile, the cleaver spun round and round, whizzing past my head—neatly slicing off the top half-inch of my left ear on the way—before burying itself into the wooden fence with a resounding *thwunk*.

I froze, convinced that if I moved, my head would fall off. "Am I still in one piece?" I whispered.

"Not quite," Shadow said, showing me the triangular chunk of ear that the cleaver had surgically removed. "But all the important parts are still attached. I think you'll live. Quick, let's beat it before he finds the rest of his knives."

We ran two blocks to a tidy bungalow on a quiet, tree-lined street.

"This is home," she said, striding up the porch steps and taking a seat on the sill of an open window. Inside the house, a middle-aged couple laughed aloud at something coming from their radio. "Do you need anything? If I bang on the window, my people will bring me some food and milk."

"No thanks. Tell me: how does my ear look?"

"Um . . . not too bad, I guess. It's only bleeding a little. I think it makes you even more handsome. It kind of . . . balances out the other one. I suppose there's a story behind that one, too."

"You could say that. Another close shave," I bragged.

She moved nearer to me, purring loudly. "You're so *exciting*, Sam. And so brave. The way you marched right in there and took those . . . those . . ."

"Sardines."

"Right. Sardines. All that, just for me."

Let's not get carried away now, I thought. Sure, I was showing off a little for a pretty girl cat, but I wanted some of those sardines for myself.

She leaned in so close that our whiskers touched, and I instinctively moved back, knocking loose the length of broomstick that had been propping up the window. In an instant, the heavy wood frame fitted with twelve panes of thick glass dropped like a guillotine—right on my tail!

For those of you reading this who *don't* have a tail, I can't possibly describe the pain I felt at that moment, but I can tell you this: my caterwauling and howling woke up every dog and baby within a three-mile radius of Shadow's house.

As I hobbled across town with a bleeding, chopped-off ear and a very sore, swollen tail, I decided that it might be best if I stayed away from female cats for a while.

Chapter 7

M y foot slipped on the last rung of the ladder that led to the roof of the Shoreliner, but somehow I managed to hold on, my fingers clutching desperately to a handhold. Accelerating down a gentle grade before leveling off and launching itself across an iron trestle bridge, the train was more than three hundred feet above the rocky riverbed. I made the stomach-churning mistake of looking down as my nails dug into the rusted steel, but when a bullet ricocheted off the side of the car just inches from my face, a shot of adrenaline rushed through my veins, giving me the sudden burst of strength I needed to drag my body over the top.

I pulled myself to my feet. There he was, three cars in

front of me and making a mad dash for the locomotive—to do what, I could only guess. Turning and seeing me, the man in the gray suit pointed his revolver and fired twice, three times, with the final shot whizzing by so close to my ear that I felt the *whoosh* of air. Undaunted, I ran after him, jumping over the spaces between cars and closing the gap between us.

"Give it up, Shipley!" he shouted. "You'll never catch us."

"You know he's right," came a voice from behind me.

I spun around to find the woman in the dark glasses, her dress snapping noisily in the wind created by the speeding train. She reached under her chin and untied her scarf, setting free her long, wavy black hair. With a dangerous smile, she lifted the blood-red scarf above her head and then let it go. Away it sailed over the edge—soaring down, down, down into the valley below.

Still smiling, she raised her gun, aiming it at my heart. Suddenly the man's hands were on my shoulders, pushing me over the edge, and I was falling . . . falling . . . falling. . . .

"Henry! Henry! Are you in there, kid?"

I opened my eyes, gasping for breath. It was too dark to see anything, but I was still alive! As I drifted in and out of consciousness, with the rest of my body trying to catch up to my brain, I noticed that my mouth was sore and dry from the gag tied around it, and the back of my head hurt worse than anything I had ever experienced. I wanted to rub it, but I soon realized that my wrists were handcuffed—to Ellie's! I couldn't make out any features in the darkness, but there was no doubt whose wrists were squeezed in the single pair of handcuffs with mine.

"How are you feeling, kid?" asked a voice inside my aching head. Sam!

"'Ere am I? Wha' happened?"

"I should have seen it coming—sorry, kid. We must have left the door open a crack. Somebody came in, saw you, and conked you one good on the head, probably with the butt of his gun. You were out cold for half an hour. Unfortunately, I had to hide under the seat, and I never got a good look at him. When he left, he turned the light off and I couldn't get to the door in time to escape and go for help. By the way, say hi to Ellie. She's been worried about you."

I grunted a hello through the gag.

"'Anks 'or 'rying to 'escue 'e," said Ellie.

"'Id they 'urt you?"

Ellie shook her head. "I'm okay. I'm 'irsty. Is your 'ead okay?"

"It 'urts, 'ut I'll live."

"So, now that everyone's awake . . . anyone for cards?" Sam asked.

"'Am! 'Top 'ooling around and 'et us out of 'ere!" I sort of shouted, which made my head hurt even more.

"All right, all right. I'm working on it, but I wasn't going any-where until I was sure you weren't dead. The bad news is that the door is the only way out of here, so I have to wait until somebody opens it. The second they do, I'll get Clarence. Okay?"

"Okay."

"What's 'e 'aying?" Ellie asked.

I explained the plan the best I could, considering I had three yards of cotton stuffed into my mouth. My head was pounding and my wrists were sore from being squeezed into the handcuffs with Ellie's. I guess the kidnappers only had one pair; my presence in the compartment was a complication that they had not planned for.

The train rocked and rolled along, reminding me of the song that Gladys and Gwendolyn had sung. From there, my mind wandered to my own family. What were Mother and Jessica doing? Part of me hoped Mother was looking for me, but another part felt guilty for worrying her. If I got out of this alive, I promised myself that I would be a better son and big brother.

The door handle jiggled, and I held my breath.

"Someone's coming," said Sam. *"I'm going to bolt when he opens that door, but I give you my word as a calico that I will be right back."*

I nodded at him and then looked at Ellie, whose eyes were glued to the door handle.

The door opened a few inches, and light from the corridor spilled into the room. There was a rustling sound, followed by a man's voice as Sam dashed over his feet and into the hallway. "Hey! What the . . . how did that cat get in here? Scared me half to death. I *hate* cats."

He opened the door just enough to let himself in and stood there quietly for a few seconds. Even though it was too dark to see his face, I was positive it was the man in the gray suit. Imagine my surprise when he turned on the light and I found myself facing the weaselly features of Reverend Perfiddle! What was *he* doing here? According to the lady in the bird hat, I should have been in the room belonging to . . . I couldn't remember, exactly—my head was still spinning.

"Okay, kiddies," he said. "Time to wake up, everyone. We're going for a little walk. Just do exactly as I say and nobody'll get hurt. Capisce?" He opened his jacket enough to give us a glimpse of his pistol—the same one that the back of my head was already quite familiar with. "Nod if you understand me."

Ellie and I nodded.

"Excellent," he said, untying the ropes around our lower legs and yanking us to our feet. Still handcuffed and facing each other, we shuffled across the room to the door, where Reverend Perfiddle held up a hand to stop us. "We're not going far. Remember, no funny stuff."

He opened it a crack and looked out. Satisfied that no one was in sight, he pulled us to a door kitty-corner from the one we'd left and roughly shoved us inside another compartment.

"Whew. Made it," he said. "Kids, say hi to your new babysitter."

Mrs. Perfiddle, sitting on the bed with her face in the shadows, gave a little wave and glared at me. "So this is the boy gumshoe who just couldn't keep his nose out of something that was *none* of his business. What are we going to do with you, little man? If there's one thing I hate, it's complications, and that's all you are to me: a complication. You're lucky—I was ready to toss you out the window of the train, but my partner is a softie. So we'll let you live—for now."

Then she stood up and it hit me: she wasn't really pregnant! It was just an act and, I guessed, merely a pillow stuffed under her blouse. But that wasn't all. When I looked a little closer, I saw another face—the face of the woman with the long red hair, the one who had not wanted to admit that the barrette belonged to her "daughter."

She must have guessed what was going through my head,

because she pinched my cheek and smiled at me. "Clever boy. I see you're putting two and two together. Maybe you're not as dumb as I thought. In fact, you're probably smarter than my partner there. Come to think of it, how *did* you know where to look for Little Miss Trust Fund? And how did you get inside? Who opened the door for you?"

An image of the hat lady flashed through my mind. She must have given me the wrong room number by accident, I thought, suddenly remembering more details of what happened before I got conked on the head. According to her, 3-B belonged to gray-suit guy and the sunglasses lady, which brought me to another question: if they weren't the kidnappers, who *were* they?

"Shhh!" said Reverend Perfiddle, his ear pressed against the door, listening for activity out in the corridor. "Someone's out there."

Mrs. Perfiddle took the pistol from beneath her pillow and jabbed it in my ribs. "Don't even *think* about making any noise," she whispered.

I heard Clarence's voice through the door. "You're sure this is the room? According to my list, it's empty."

Faintly, sounding as if he were miles away, Sam's voice answered inside my head. *"Yes, I'm sure. 3-B."*

Clarence knocked, waited a few seconds, and then knocked again. "Henry? You in there? Henry? Ellie?"

Reverend Perfiddle's eyes bugged out of his head, and he turned to his wife with a befuddled look. "How the heck does he know?" he hissed. "Nobody saw me! I swear!" He stared at me. "Did you tell someone where you were going?"

I shook my head. Even if I *had*, I wouldn't have told him.

"You *idiot*," snarled Mrs. Perfiddle. "Somebody must have seen *something*. I knew that salesman story would never hold up. That's what I get for trusting you. All right, what's done is done. That's the conductor's voice, for sure. Who's with him?"

"I can't tell. Can't hear anyone else," said Reverend Perfiddle.

"Use your key," said Sam. *"Trust me; they're inside."*

The distinctive sound of Judge Ambrose's shoes *clack*ed down the corridor.

"I know who *that* is," said the minister as the sound slowed and then stopped outside the door to 3-B.

So did Sam. *"Wonderful. How's he going to try to kill me this time?"*

"All right, Mr. Nockwood, I came, like you asked," the judge blustered. "Now, are you going to tell me what this has to do with that . . . barrette, or whatever it is, that you found? Whose compartment is this? And what is *that* doing here?"

It wasn't hard to figure out that Sam was the *that* Judge Ambrose found so offensive.

Clarence ignored the reference to Sam. "Officially, this is an empty compartment. We had a few unsold rooms this trip. However, I believe that Ellie Strasbourg is inside."

"Based on what information?"

I grinned, thinking of the real answer to that question: a little kitty-cat told me. The smile on Ellie's face assured me that she was thinking the same thing.

"I . . . received a tip," Clarence fibbed, "from someone who . . . would prefer to remain anonymous. That . . . and the barrette that Henry Shipley found, which has been identified by Mrs. Strasbourg as Ellie's . . ."

"Ludicrous!" cried the judge. "The girl was taken off the train. I thought we went over this, several times! Well, let's get on with it. Open the door."

"Okay, I'm going in," said Clarence.

We all heard the jangling of keys, followed by several seconds of silence.

"This is impossible," said Sam. *"They were right there! They were handcuffed to each other and tied up so they couldn't move their legs."*

"You old fool!" cried the judge. "Wasting my time like this. Mrs. Strasbourg has put her trust in me to make sure that the necklace is ready for the drop-off. Please don't bother me again with your imbecilic . . . follies. The next time you want to go on a wild-goose chase, I suggest you take your *cat*." He stomped off, sounding like a team of Clydesdales and laughing rudely at poor Clarence.

"Clarence, you have to believe me," Sam pleaded. *"I saw them."*

"But you didn't see the kidnapper, and now nobody is going to believe anything I say."

"Oh, don't let that overinflated zeppelin get to you. You can't give up on me now. Whoever the kidnapper is, they have to be nearby. They had to move two kids without accidentally bumping into anyone, and that's not easy to do on a full train. Come on; let's check some of these other rooms."

"How many would you like me to check? I know who's in this one, and this one, and that one, and Mrs. Perfiddle is in that one. I don't care what you say, I'm not going to bother her. Poor woman is about to have a baby."

"Who is he *talking* to?" Mrs. Perfiddle asked, digging the barrel of the pistol farther into my ribs.

"The baby is the least of her problems," said Sam. *"How'd you like to live with Reverend Perfiddle? The man's a complete twit."* Part of me wished that the twit could have heard that for himself as Sam continued. *"Fine. You go back and keep an eye*

on the judge. I saw the way he looked at that necklace. You humans have been known to do some pretty foolish things over a hunk of rock like that. Of course, I'm not a hundred percent certain that the judge is human. I'm staying here until I see what I need to see."

Reverend Perfiddle removed his ear from the door and lit a cigarette. "I think they're gone. Whew, that was close. If I hadn't moved when I did . . ."

"Yeah, yeah, you're a regular Albert Wisenstein," said Mrs. Perfiddle. "How much longer to Dunkirk? I'm going stir-crazy in here with these brats."

"Not long. In fact, I need to get moving if I'm going to . . ."

"Shut up! These two don't need to hear all the details. Just *go*."

Mrs. Perfiddle was in such a hurry to close the door as he was leaving that she shut it on his fingers. He howled in pain and let loose a string of words that would have made me gasp if I hadn't been gagged.

"Quiet!" she snarled, locking the door behind him. "Nincompoop."

Even though I was a *little* bit scared, I couldn't help laughing, and neither could Ellie.

"Oh, you think that's funny, do you?" Mrs. Perfiddle said, attempting to be serious but unable to hold back her own smile. She patted Ellie on the head, as if she were petting a dog. "Kid, take my advice. Don't get married. When we started going out, everybody told me how lucky I was to find a fella like him. Believe me, if anybody's lucky, it's him. I'd say he's an imbecile, but that's not fair to the imbeciles of the world. He'd have to get quite a bit smarter before they'd let him into the club. So when you two kids grow up and Prince Charming here asks you to marry him, run in the other direction as fast as your legs will take you."

Ellie grunted to get Mrs. Perfiddle's attention. "Ah-er!"

"Huh?"

"Ah! Er! I 'eed ah-er!"

"Ohhh. *Water*. I guess that would be all right." She started to untie Ellie's gag. "Don't forget, I still have a gun pointed at you."

Without taking her eyes off us, she filled a cup and handed it to Ellie, who drank it in one gulp and asked for more. She downed a second cupful and stared up at Mrs. Perfiddle.

"I know who you are. I recognized you right away from the picture in the post office. You and your partner are Connie and Ty. Kind of like Bonnie and Clyde, but not nearly as famous. Or as smart, I think. You're never going to get away with this, you know. I told a *bunch* of people on this train about you and they're going to catch you."

Mrs. Perfiddle—Connie—didn't look too worried.

"Sure, kid. But you see, it's almost over, and I *am* going to get away with it, even though I'm stuck with Ty, who is dumber than a sack of dead chickens. It was his fault the FBI even got that picture of us. The whole thing was his idea. Once he got his hands on those machine guns, we just had to pose like Bonnie and Clyde, he said. You want to know a secret? He's afraid to shoot the thing! Tried it once, and almost shot his own foot off."

Ellie pointed at the pistol in Connie's hand. "I'll bet you don't even know how to use that. Have you ever shot anybody? Or do you just go around scaring people with it? You know what? I'll bet it's not even loaded."

Connie lifted Ellie's chin with the cold steel barrel of the pistol. "Unless you want to find out the hard way, you ought to shut up, kid. You should consider yourself lucky. You're going to get out of this with hardly a scratch. All your rich mommy and daddy have to do is hand over a little necklace. Big deal. They'll buy another one just like it. Except . . . it really is one of a kind, isn't it? I guess mommy will have to—" She stopped suddenly, holding up a hand to silence Ellie, even though she wasn't the one talking. "Someone's out there," she said, pointing her gun at the door.

"*Mrrraaaa,*" said Sam. "*Mrrraaaaaaaa.*"

"What was that?" cried Connie, almost jumping out of her skin.

"Sam!" said Ellie.

Connie waved the gun wildly. "Shut up! Who's Sam?" It took a few moments for the truth to hit her, and when it did, she laughed at herself. "It's the conductor's cat, isn't it? You know, I always liked cats, but I'm allergic to them."

Sam's voice rang inside my head again: *"Henry! Are you in there with Ellie? If you can't talk, stomp your foot or bang your head against the wall so I can hear, okay? On the count of three. One . . . two . . . three!"*

I lifted both feet off the ground and brought them down as hard as I could on the floor. With all the usual noise of the train, it wasn't very loud, but it did the job.

"Hey! What are you doing?" Connie asked. "Sit still." She opened the door a few inches and peeked outside. "Here, kitty, kitty. Come inside. I guess it's okay as long as I don't touch you."

Sam poked his head inside. *"I need to talk to you, kid. You think it's safe?"*

I nodded, and Sam's lanky body slinked inside.

"You are one ugly cat, I have to tell you," said Connie. "Somebody dipped you in a bucket of ugly. Twice. Poor little girl."

"Sam's a *boy*," said Ellie. "He's not ugly—he's *beautiful*."

Connie refolded Ellie's gag and held it up for her to

see. "Goes to show how much you know, Little Miss Foo-Foo Private School. That's a calico, and all calicoes are girls. Even Ty knows that. And if she's beautiful, I'm Miss America."

Smiling at her own joke, she carefully retied the gag around Ellie's head. When she finished, Ellie smiled at me, her eyes twinkling; she knew that Sam was there for a reason.

Connie's face suddenly changed. "Aaa-chooo! Aaa-chooo! I knew it. That stupid cat has to go."

"No! 'Et 'im 'tay!" said Ellie.

Sam glared menacingly at Connie. *"Mrrraaaaaaaa. I'm going to dip you in a bucket of something a whole lot worse than ugly when this is all over,"* he promised.

Seeing that would almost make the bump on my head worthwhile, I thought.

"Reverend Picklebarrel, or whoever he is, led me to you," said Sam. *"I guessed that you were still in this car, so I just waited around, watching and listening. When he came out of the room, stomping and cussing because he'd smashed his fingers, I didn't think anything of it. Got a good laugh out of it, if you want to know the truth. Figured he was taking care of his pregnant wife, right? But then he made a big mistake. That weasel actually flicked his cigarette butt at me! I thought about shredding that cheap suit of*

his, but then I realized something important: the cigarette butt was exactly like the one that I saw in the ashtray of the salesman's room. It was a hand-rolled cigarette, but not like any other I've ever seen. It was nearly perfect, almost as if a machine had made it. And the paper was different, too—do you remember? Lighter color than a cigar, but not white, either, and I just knew . . . well, I can tell you the rest later. You're probably ready to get out of here. I'm going to get the cavalry, but it may take a while. I have to convince Clarence that dear Mrs. Pimpleman here is no more pregnant than I am, and that's going to take some talking. Hang in there, kid. And let Ellie know we're coming for her."

It was my turn to grunt for water.

Connie shook her head and then sneezed three times. "Sorry, handsome, but you've only been tied up for a few minutes. If you're going to sneak around rescuing people, you're going to have to toughen up. Aaa-chooo! I have to get rid of that cat." Before she got around to chasing Sam out, though, curiosity got the better of her and she changed her mind about removing my gag. "You know, I have to admit that I am a little bit confused: How *did* you know where to find her? How did you even know that she was still on the train?" She reached behind my head and untied the handkerchief.

"Water first," I demanded.

Connie filled the cup and watched me drink. "Okay,

you've had your water. Tell me what I want to know. *Quietly.*"

I thought about it for a moment. I could tell the truth—that I had thought the porter was letting me into the compartment belonging to Mr. and Mrs. Gray Suit, and that it was dumb luck that I stumbled into Ellie. (Had the bird-hat lady given me the wrong room number by accident? I honestly did not know the answer to that question.) But why should I give Connie the satisfaction? Why not let her think that I had outsmarted the famous criminal duo of Connie and Ty?

I pursed my lips and shook my head. (My father would have keelhauled me if he'd seen me acting that way.) "I changed my mind. I don't feel like telling you. You wouldn't believe me, anyway. Oh, all right, I'll admit it: it was all Sam! Don't let his looks fool you. He's smarter than Rin Tin Tin. As soon as you let him out of here, he's going to go get help. He'll probably tap out a message in Morse code using his paws. You can relax now, Ellie. We'll be rescued in no time."

"*That's quick thinking, kid,*" said Sam. "*We'll make a detective out of you yet.*"

"Ha-ha. Very funny," said Connie. "You ought to be in pictures. Maybe when you get to Chicago, you and Rin Tin Ugly can just keep going, all the way to Hollywood."

Sam scratched at the door. *"Mrrraaaa."*

Connie laughed again. "Well, I guess I'd better let him go. I forgot—he has to tell the coppers where we've got you and Miss Moneybags stashed away." She listened at the door and then opened it enough to let Sam out. "Go on, then. Run, Sam, run! Go get help! Good riddance to you, you old bag of fleas." She closed the door, laughing heartily at her little joke until she was overcome by a string of six sneezes.

Before the door closed, though, Sam had turned around and given her one final, evil look. *"Oh, I am going to have so much fun watching you go down for this. Nobody messes with the Shoreliner."*

At that moment, up in the locomotive, the Shoreliner's engineer sounded the horn as we approached the next station, but we weren't slowing down. Dunkirk was too small to be a regular stop for the Shoreliner, and we zoomed past the platform at sixty miles per hour.

"Dunkirk," said Connie, reading the station signs. "That's the drop-off point. The Blue Streak is almost mine, at last. I've been dreaming about this day for ages. Sorry, kid, but I have to gag you again. Almost time for my big exit. But don't despair! Rin Tin Ugly will show up with the sheriff just in time to save the day. That's how it always happens in the movies, right?" She seemed to enjoy tying the handkerchief around my head, roughly shoving the cloth between my teeth.

Then she fixed her hair and makeup and stuffed a pillow under her blouse, and just like that she was poor, pregnant Mrs. Perfiddle again.

"Not bad, huh?" she said. "Even I almost believe I'm 'in a delicate condition.' Ha! Men are such fools! They see a pregnant lady and they go completely soft. I guess I shouldn't complain. Their stupidity is going to make me rich."

As she pulled on a lightweight overcoat, someone knocked twice on the door. "Speaking of stupid," she said, unlocking the door for her partner in crime, "here's the king now."

Ty could barely contain his excitement. "I got it!" he shouted, twirling the Blue Streak on his index finger, the jewels sparkling in the overhead light.

Connie slapped him hard across the face and screeched at him, "What are you doing? Don't show them, you . . . you imbecile! Arghh! What is wrong with you? Can't you, just *once*, stick to the plan?"

Ty rubbed his face where Connie's handprint looked as if it had been painted on, while I tried to sort out what had happened. The plan, as far as we knew, had been to put the necklace into an official US mailbag, which was then

171

supposed to be "picked up" by the hook at the Dunkirk station. From there, we assumed, a member of their gang would retrieve it, and afterward, they would meet up together at their secret hideout.

So how had it ended up in Ty's grimy hands?

"You're not the boss of me," he whined. "In case you forgot, we're *partners*. I'm sick of you treating me like I'm some hayseed who don't know one end of a gun from the other. And right now, it's *me* who's got the cabbage."

"In case *you* forgot," said Connie, poking him in the chest with her index finger, "when Daddy and I rescued you from that one-horse town, you *were* a hayseed. If it weren't for me, you'd still be shoveling cow manure or serving time in the county jail for stealing that old jalopy. So from now on, when I tell you to do something, you do it, no questions asked. Is that clear, *Tyler*?"

His eyes got watery, and for a second I thought he was going to cry, but he pulled himself together before any tears fell. "It's clear," he sniffed.

Don't Call Me Samantha

THE ALMOST ENTIRELY TRUE
AUTOBIOGRAPHY OF LANTERN SAM

I Earn a New Name

I didn't quite make it back to Linesville. Not that time, anyway.

After the fiasco with Shadow and the Sardines (wouldn't that be a great name for a nightclub act?), I was desperate for some peace and quiet, and a good night's sleep. About halfway between Andover and Linesville, I stopped at a farm-house and crawled into a wagon full of hay and fell into a deep slumber.

A few hours later, that wagon rumbled to life beneath me and I woke with a start, digging my way to the top of the pile in time to see a sign that read, YOU ARE LEAVING ANDOVER— COME BACK SOON! Up ahead, a shiny new Ford pulled the wagon and yours truly north on Route 7, away from the Dilly farm, which lay to the east. I considered making a run for it the first time we slowed down, but then I thought: what if this hay wagon is Fate's way of telling me it's not the right time to return to the farm in Linesville? I burrowed into the hay and went back to sleep.

The sound of a train whistle woke me a little later, and it took me only a moment to realize where I was: the train station in Ashtabula, where I had said goodbye to Butch. Chugging up to the platform at that very moment was a locomotive with the name Lake Erie Shoreliner emblazoned across its nose and a dozen Pullman cars behind—a most impressive sight, indeed.

"Ashtabula!" roared the conductor, stepping gracefully from a sleeper car as the train came to a stop. "All aboard the Shoreliner for New York City!"

The Shoreliner! New York City! For a small-town cat like me, it was a dream come true. All I had to do was find a way to weasel my way aboard. The conductor looked like a friendly sort, so I ran across the platform toward him. Of course, I had to keep in mind that some humans, even a few who *look* nice, don't like cats—hard as *that* may be to believe.

The conductor saw me and smiled. "Why, hey there, little fellow."

I liked him already—he called me a fellow, rather than

assuming I was a girl. "Hope you've got room for one more," I said, certainly *not* expecting a reply.

I don't know how I knew, but somehow I knew he *had* heard me. Realizing that there was no one else nearby, he stopped and stared at me, his head cocked to one side.

"Is that a yes?" I asked.

"Well, dog my cat!" he said. "That's the darnedest thing I ever . . . why, I suppose it is a yes. Come on aboard. I was just about to have a little snack. Do you like sardines?"

"Mrrraaa. We're going to get along just fine," I said. "My name is Sam, by the way."

"I'm Clarence. Clarence Nockwood."

Call it whatever you like—fate, coincidence, destiny—but I was meant to be on that platform in Ashtabula that day. Sure, I give Clarence a hard time every now and again, but all in all, he's a good egg, and he *did* save my life. Well, one of my lives, anyway. It happened like this:

I had been with Clarence and the Shoreliner a little over a year, riding the rails back and forth between New York City and Chicago. On his rare days off, Clarence took me to his little farm outside of Dunkirk, New York—a pretty town on Lake Erie where I could admire the view of the lake without having to go near the water.

Clarence's wife, like millions of others, had died from the

flu back in 1918, so when the Depression hit, he left the farm in the able hands of his son, Norman, and went to work for the railroad. When we came back for visits, Clarence always seemed a little sad; whether he still missed his wife, missed life on the farm, or simply hated being away from the Shoreliner, I was never entirely sure.

In the evenings, after the chores were finished and the dinner plates washed, Clarence and Norman drove into Dunkirk to visit old friends. They would all meet at the Boxcar Tavern, an old railroad boxcar that a retired conductor had bought and turned into a bar back in the days before Prohibition. It wasn't much to look at, but the drinks were cheap and the bartender was a cheerful but foulmouthed sailor named François, who boasted that he had the same number of teeth and ex-wives as he had fingers—nine.

On one especially frigid, snowy night, while Clarence and Norman sat on their stools listening to another of François's far-fetched tales, I went in search of someplace warm to curl up for a few hours. The potbelly stove in one corner of the car looked promising, but there was a semicircle of men seated around it, and they didn't look like they were the type to want to share with a cat, if you know what I mean. And even if they had made room for me, I knew better than to risk it. You see, every customer at the Boxcar (except Clarence) chewed tobacco—a filthy habit if ever there was one.

A sign over the bar warned them to spit into the brass spit-toons near the stove, but their aim was downright terrible, and most of the time they didn't even bother—they just spat on the floor, or onto anything (or anyone) who happened to be in the way.

In the opposite corner of the car were two unoccupied tables. At the center of each flickered an authentic railroad lantern, so I hightailed it to the one farthest from the spit-ters and jumped aboard. The lantern's wick was turned down low, so it wasn't very bright, but it still gave off a surprising amount of heat, which was all I was interested in. I lay down on the table, curled my lanky body around that miniature furnace, and drifted off to dreamland.

My memory of what happened next is a little fuzzy, so I've had to rely on Clarence to fill in some of the gory details, especially those leading up to the moment I found myself buried in a snowdrift outside the Boxcar Tavern.

According to Clarence, it was François who first noticed something odd.

"What the devil's that *smell*?" he asked the men around the potbelly stove. "I've told you a hundred times: you can't take your shoes off in here. Those feet o' yours'll kill somebody."

"It ain't us," said one. "We all got our shoes on. You sure *yours* are on? Seems to me it's your feet what peeled the paint off the ceiling."

"Holy cats!" said another. "It ain't feet—it's that dang cat of Clarence's!"

In my dreams, I was a guest at a country estate, curled up on a hearthrug before a blazing fire after a long day of hunting.

In reality, I was on fire.

Whether someone intentionally turned up the wick on the lantern (as I have always suspected) or not, we will never know. No one was willing to admit to tampering with the lantern, and at the moment it would have happened, I was too busy enjoying my fantasy life to notice if someone was trying to kill me. Whatever the case, *somehow* that stupid lantern got so hot that the fur on my belly started to smoke—and not just a little. Clarence said that when he first looked over at me, so much smoke was pouring off me that he couldn't believe there were no flames.

"Water!" he bellowed at François.

In the meantime, a couple of the potbelly stove warriors pushed me away from the lantern. I opened my eyes just in time to watch the first of them dump the entire disgusting contents of a spittoon over my belly, followed a moment later by a second man, whose spittoon was filled even closer to the top than the first.

Dripping with tobacco juice and who knows what else, I

was too shocked to fight back. "Ack! Eeuuckkk! Aaauggghhhh. What is—"

Before I could finish cursing at them, Clarence reached me with the bucket of soapy water that François kept behind the bar and dumped *it* over me. Then he carried me to the front door by the scruff of my neck and tossed me into the nearest snowdrift to make sure that the fire was really out.

The temperature outside the Boxcar Tavern that night was six degrees below zero, so it doesn't take much imagination to picture me as I crawled out of that drift. In seconds, all that tobacco juice and soapy water froze so solidly that I could barely move, and I had to be rescued by Clarence once more. He took me back inside and held me directly in front of the potbelly stove until I thawed out enough that he could start to clean me up with François's bar rag, which smelled only slightly better than the contents of the two spittoons I was wearing.

Clarence looked down at me and smiled as the fur on my belly came out in soggy, charred clumps. "I think you just used up one of your lives, Sam, old boy. Maybe two. You know, I think we'll call you *Lantern* Sam from now on. Has a nice ring to it."

Chapter 8

For the next twenty minutes, nobody in that stuffy, crowded room said a word. Connie and Ty weren't speaking to each other, and with our mouths crammed full of hankies, Ellie and I didn't exactly have a choice in the matter. The *clackety-clackety-clackety* of the wheels and the gentle rocking of the car threatened to lull me to sleep; it was well past my bedtime and it had been a long day. All I wanted to do was close my eyes and magically wake up in my own bed, with the smell of griddle cakes and bacon filling the air.

What had happened to Sam? It was hard to believe that it was taking so long to find Clarence and get him to open the door. In all the excitement and confusion, I had lost track of the time, but I knew it had to be well after nine o'clock; that dinner with Mother and Jessica was only a distant memory. Meanwhile, I was beginning to imagine the "wow finish" to the story: Clarence and some of the porters breaking down the door in a hail of machine-gun fire, maybe even a hand grenade or two. Sam swinging in on a rope, his own tommy gun blazing. Connie and Ty refusing to give up without a fight, bullets whizzing past my ears in both directions. At least that's how it would happen in *Dick Tracy*.

I had skinned my knee a few days earlier, and the scab was starting to itch. With a little effort, I was able to reach the area with my handcuffed hands, which is when I felt something in my pants pocket: the sardine can key. *If* I could get it out of the pocket without Connie or Ty noticing anything, I knew that it would be possible to open handcuffs with it—at least that's what I'd read in *Captain Billy's Whiz Bang*.

Ty checked his watch about every ten seconds, it seemed. He was the one to break the silence. "Just a few more minutes to North East. Finally. I can't wait to get off this bucket of bolts. You ready?"

"Been ready," said Connie. "How about these two? Double-check all the ropes and make sure those cuffs are on nice and tight. Don't need any surprises."

Ty lifted our wrists and tugged on the cuffs.

"Ow," I said as he tried to squeeze my hand through the opening. I was glad I hadn't gotten the key out of my pocket.

"They're not going anywhere," he announced.

"Maybe we ought to give them both a shot of that special beddy-bye juice, just to be sure. They'd sleep all the way to Chicago."

I shook my head as hard as I could. "No! 'E'll 'e 'uiet!"

Connie smiled sweetly at me. Well, she *tried* to smile sweetly. It actually came out looking more like a sneer. "Okay, kid, I'm going to trust you. Once we're off this train, it's not going to matter anyway. Well, you kids have a nice ride to Chicago. I'm sure they'll find you in the morning when they come through to clean everything. That is, unless Rin Tin Tin comes to rescue you first. Oh, sorry . . . looks like he forgot you." She laughed in my face and turned toward the door.

"Is Rin Tin Tin really on the train?" asked Ty, closing the door as they stepped into the hall.

With Connie and Ty out of sight, my thoughts turned to the sardine key in my pants pocket. Somehow I *had* to get it out, but it wasn't going to be easy. Not only were our wrists squeezed together into one pair of handcuffs, but the chain also ran through the steel frame of the seat. I couldn't move my hands more than a few inches in any direction, so I had no choice—I had to get the pocket closer to my hands. To do that, we had to twist our bodies around so that our faces were mere inches apart. If someone had walked in at that moment, I would have dropped dead from embarrassment, because it looked like I was trying to kiss Ellie. Blindly, I pushed my fingertips into the pocket and fished around for the key, which, naturally, had dropped into the deepest, farthest corner.

After an eternity in that awkward, uncomfortable position, I was able to get one finger on the key and slowly drag it upward until I could get it between my fingertips and start to pull it to safety. I finally held it up triumphantly for Ellie to see.

"Wha's 'at?"

"'Ardine 'ey." With my right hand, I stuck the end of the key into the lock of the handcuff that held my left and Ellie's right hand and started wiggling it around. I'd seen people escape from handcuffs a million times in the pictures— how hard could it be?

I wiggled. I jiggled. I twisted and I turned, and nothing happened. Discouraged, I took a deep breath, relaxed my fingers, and tried again. Still nothing. Maybe it wasn't as simple as they made it seem in the movies.

"'Et 'e 'ry," said Ellie, holding her hand out for the key.

"Okay, 'ut 'on't 'rop it," I warned. The Shoreliner was

speeding toward its next stop, and time was running out. Doggone that Sam—where was he?

Ellie's face was a picture of concentration. Since she was right-handed, too, she decided to tackle the cuff around her left wrist first. She put the key in, gave it a quarter turn to the right, and . . . *presto,* the cuff dropped open! She looked over at me, her eyes huge—almost as big as mine!

"I did it!" she cried after ripping the handkerchief from her face. "Oh, that feels so much better! I can't believe it worked. How did you know you could open handcuffs with a sardine key?"

With my free hand, I yanked the gag from my mouth and threw it to the floor. "I'll tell you later . . . but first, do the other one. I'm going to need both hands to untie these knots."

She took the key in her left hand and started to work on the other cuff, fully expecting that it would open as easily as the first. That turned out to be wishful thinking. A minute went by, then two, and our wrists remained bound together.

"Let me try again," I said. She passed the key to me without protest, but I didn't have her magic touch. No matter what I did, that cuff remained stubbornly clamped to our wrists. "We're going to have to leave it on for now. We're running out of time. C'mon—together we can untie the ropes. We have to stop those two before we get to the next station, or we're never going to see them or your mom's necklace again."

My right hand and Ellie's left hand picked at Ty's sloppily tied granny knots (the kind that Father would have scolded me for tying), and within five minutes we were free—except for the handcuff that joined us.

"Let's get out of here," I said, tossing the last bit of rope aside.

"I have to see Mother," she said. "She must be so . . ."

"We will," I promised. "But first, you have to come with me—to prove everything to them. They won't believe me. They don't believe anything I say."

Ellie nodded, but I noticed that her eyes were a little watery. I think that it was all finally starting to sink in—her being knocked out and kidnapped, the Blue Streak, her mother, everything that had happened in the few short hours I had known her.

"It'll be all right," I said. "Nobody's going to hurt you now. And don't forget, we have Lantern Sam on our side, *if* we can find him."

Oh, we found him all right.

We burst through the door and had started to race down the hall when I heard that familiar voice in my head.

"Henry! Is that you?"

As I screeched to a halt, forgetting momentarily that I was still attached to Ellie, she flew right into me, and we both tumbled to the floor in a tangle of arms and legs.

"What are you *doing*?" said Ellie. "Why did you stop?"

"I heard Sam. He's in one of these rooms." I helped her to her feet, and we quickly shook off the bumps and bruises we'd gained. "Sam! Can you hear me?"

"You don't have to shout," he said calmly. *"Just get me out of here!"*

"Out of where?"

"4-C. Hurry."

"Why'd you go in there?"

"I—didn't—choose—to come in here, you dolt. A feeble-minded . . . human picked me up and carried me inside. Can I help it if people find me irresistible?"

"What's going on?" Ellie asked. "Where is he?"

I put my ear to the door of 4-C. "He's in here. I'm not sure why."

"Are there people in there?"

"Will you two please stop wasting time and knock on the door?" said Sam, getting very testy.

I knocked twice.

"Who is it?" A man's voice, not at all friendly sounding.

"Henry Shipley," I said.

"What do you want?"

"I'm, uh, looking for my cat. I just wondered if you've seen him. He's a calico—"

The door burst open and I found myself looking up at the face of the man in the gray suit.

"You!" He pointed his finger accusingly at me and then yanked me into the room, with poor, bruised Ellie stumbling in after me. He blocked our exit with his body and demanded, "Who are you working for? Why are you handcuffed? What's going on?"

"I—I, uh—wh-what do you mean?" I stammered.

"Don't play dumb with me, sonny boy. You know who *that* is?" He pointed at the woman with the dark glasses. She was staring out the window at the dim lights of distant farmhouses while she absentmindedly petted Sam, who was perched on her lap.

"N-no," I said. "I've never seen her before—I mean, before I got on the train."

Ellie's face lit up. "You're Madeline Parker! I almost didn't recognize you with those glasses. Shouldn't you be in New York? Don't you have a show tonight?"

Miss Parker removed the glasses, revealing her improbably blue eyes for the first time, and smiled at Ellie.

In addition to being fascinated by her eyes, I must have looked confused, because Ellie felt the need to tell me more. "She's only the most famous actress on Broadway. She's won just about every award you can win, and—"

Mr. Gray Suit poked me with his finger again. "Don't act like you don't know who she is! Do you think I just fell off the turnip truck? Do you?"

"T-turnip truck?" I said, getting more confused by the minute.

"I saw you talking to your friend with the funny hat— Phyllis Finkleman, the *gossip* columnist, as if you didn't know that already! I have to give that crazy dame credit, though. This time she's really outdone herself, following us halfway across the country for her little scoop. And by the way, when you see her, tell her I said that hat is the most hideous thing I've ever seen. So, how much is she paying you to snoop on us? Where's your spy camera? Let me see those handcuffs. Are they even real? Or are you just using them to get my sympathy, so I'll let down my guard? And the next thing you know, Maddy's on the front page of your paper. Why can't you people just leave us alone?"

I backed away, utterly bewildered. "Look, mister . . . are you talking about the lady with the yellow birds on her hat? Because I did talk to her, but it was about—" I cut myself off, remembering that I *had* talked to her about them, although it wasn't for the reason he thought. "We're not working for her, I swear. This is Ellie Strasbourg—the girl who was kidnapped! You *must* have heard about that. I know it sounds crazy, but after the conductor and I figured out that she was still on the train, I thought you two were the kidnappers. But I found her and we used a sardine can key to open one of the cuffs and escape, but if we don't find the conductor and Judge Ambrose before we get to the next stop, the kidnappers are going to get away!"

"Whoa! Take a breath, kid," said Sam. "Now, go back to the part where you mentioned something about a sardine can. Because I'm thinking if there's a key, there must be sardines nearby. Are you holding out on me, kid? Because if you are . . ."

Mr. Gray Suit, still blocking the door, crossed his arms and jutted his chin out at me, and I missed the rest of what Sam said. "If that's true, and you're in such a big hurry, how do you explain your taking the time to look for your cat?"

"Ooh, that's a really good question," said Sam, chuckling inside my head. "I can't wait to hear your answer."

"We . . . I . . . need him," I said. "He's . . . Sam's just really . . . important, but I can't tell you why. . . . Can I *please* explain later? We need to find the conductor right away. When this train reaches the next stop at Ripley, they're going to hop off and get away with . . . with everything."

A smiling Miss Parker held up her hand to stop me. "Wait. Back up a second. You thought *we* were the kidnappers? What on earth made you think that?"

"I guess you looked guilty. Ellie told me that she recognized two criminals on the train, but before she could point them out to me, somebody nabbed her. Every time I saw you, you were wearing dark glasses, and you were both always looking over your shoulders. And you," I added, pointing at Mr. Gray Suit, "you couldn't stop playing with your wedding ring. I thought maybe it was a fake, and you were just pretending to be married. And then that lady in the hat said something about you two and how you were in hiding. . . ."

"We're not in hiding!" said Mr. Gray Suit, getting more and more agitated. "When I get my hands on her, I'm going to—"

Miss Parker stood up, holding Sam to her chest. "Darling, relax. The cat's out of the bag, so to speak. A big ol' lanky calico cat named Sam, to be precise. By the time we get to Chicago, the whole world is going to know that we're married. And so what? When we get there, I think we should stand on the roof of the train and announce it to the world. And another thing—so what if your play opened and closed on the same night. It doesn't mean it's a bad play; in fact, it's brilliant. The public just isn't ready for

Alabama Woodward . . . yet. But don't worry, they'll come around. All the controversy will blow over in a few days, and then no one will care because the Phyllis Finklemans of the world will have found someone else to bother. Now step aside and let this nice young man out of this compartment before he has a heart attack." She gave Sam a nudge out of her lap. "You too, gorgeous."

"Alabama Woodward?" said Sam, suddenly looking up at Mr. Gray Suit with respect. *"Henry, my boy, we are in the presence of one of the truly great playwrights of our time. A true genius. Mark my words: Mr. Woodward will go down in history as the William Shakespeare of the Great Depression. Last summer, I saw a production of his play* Sardines and Sixpence *because—well, I think you can probably guess why I went to see it—and it was brilliant! Mrrraaa. I could go for some sardines right now. I don't suppose—"*

"Sam!" I shouted. "I don't care if he *is* William Shakespeare! We need to go right *now*, and we're not stopping for *sardines*!"

There was absolute silence in the compartment as everyone froze. Baffled by my outburst, they stared, mouthing the word *sardines* and thinking, no doubt, that I had lost my mind.

Alabama Woodward stepped aside and opened the door without making a sound.

"We have to hurry," I said, pulling Ellie toward the dining car and the sounds of Gladys and Gwendolyn.

"What was that about sardines?" she asked.

We burst into the dining car as the final notes of a song I didn't recognize still hung in the air. On the way in, we almost knocked down Phyllis Finkleman, whose hands were poised to be the first to clap for the Henshaw Sisters.

The crowd parted and we found ourselves in the center of the room, with thirty pairs of eyes on us.

"That's her!" said one man. "That's the Strasbourg girl!"

"I thought the kidnappers took her off the train," a woman remarked.

"Where's the conductor? Where's Clarence?" I asked, my eyes scanning the room. "Has anybody seen him?"

The train's whistle blew as we went around a bend and started down a long, gentle incline.

I spun around, and my eyes landed on Connie and Ty, who shared a nervous look. As Ty slowly stood up, I watched his hand reach inside his jacket where he kept his gun.

"Uh-oh."

"What's going on?" said Sam. *"Pick me up. I can't see anything from down—mrrraaa! See you later, kid."*

"Wh-what? Where are you going? Find Clarence!" I

twisted my head around to see what had scared him off and found myself face to giant red face with Judge Ambrose.

"What's the meaning of this?" he boomed. "What's going on here?"

Ellie and I lifted our handcuffed wrists to show him.

"I found her. This is Ellie. She was still on the train, just like Clarence said. Only *you* didn't believe him."

The judge took a step back, and his usually bright pink cheeks and nose lightened a few shades. He was definitely a bit shocked by my success.

"What do you mean, you *found* her? Who gave you permission to even be *looking* for her? *Where* did you find her? And *why* are you two handcuffed together?"

"It was *them*," I announced, pointing with my free hand across the car at Connie and Ty, still known to everyone else as Reverend and Mrs. Perfiddle. "They did it. They took her. And they did *this*."

"Who? Who took her?" Judge Ambrose blustered.

"Reverend Perfiddle and his wife," I said. "They're big phonies, *and* they're crooks! Their real names are Connie and Ty, and they're wanted by the FBI. I *told* you that Ellie recognized two criminals when they got on the train. It was *them*."

The crowd of passengers who had been enjoying the

music of Gladys and Gwendolyn eyed Connie and Ty suspiciously.

A smile formed in the corner of the judge's mouth, which then quickly turned into a huge, toothy grin. He threw that basketball-sized head of his back and let loose a roar of laughter so loud that Ellie and I both flinched.

"Haw-haw-haw! Good one, kid. You're a regular Groucho Marx." He addressed the crowd: "Folks, we have great news! We found Ellie Strasbourg, and she's unharmed. We need to get her back to her mother's compartment right away."

"What about *them*?" asked Phyllis Finkleman, pointing at Connie and Ty and then taking two steps toward them. She didn't seem to be afraid of anything, or anyone. "The boy said that they're responsible. Are you going to arrest them?"

"Madam, I think you should leave this to the men," said Judge Ambrose. "It's obvious that there's been a mistake made here. The girl is in shock. She doesn't know what happened. Here's what I think happened, and it's what I've been saying all along, from the moment she disappeared. I'm still not sure how or why, but this boy has been involved in this little plot from the very beginning, all the way up to his scrawny little neck. Slowly but surely, we've been closing in on him, and when he knew we were about to pounce, he handcuffed himself to her and then ran in here shouting crazy stories about the good Reverend Perfiddle and his poor wife. Folks, take a good look at them. Do they look like criminals to you? Mrs. Perfiddle, I apologize for this inexcusable intrusion, but would you please stand up for a moment?"

Connie put on a performance worthy of a headlining role on Broadway. Slowly, dramatically, she rose to her feet, turning her enormous belly sideways for the full effect. And then, as if that wasn't theatrical enough, she "fainted," falling into the outstretched arms of the oh-so-innocent-looking Ty.

Women gasped. Men harrumphed. Both groups clucked disapprovingly at me.

"You see what I mean, my friends?" said Ambrose, puffing himself up. "Now, help me reunite this little girl with her mother. Look at the poor thing. She's too frightened to speak!"

The crowd started to close in around Ellie and me. Even Phyllis Finkleman looked at me suspiciously.

"She's faking! Criminy, it's not even a real baby!" I cried. "It's just a *pillow*. I saw her put it inside her blouse."

"Shut up, kid," said the man who thought I was shushing him in the lounge a few hours earlier.

"Where is his mother?" his wife asked. "She should be ashamed."

"What he needs is a few lashes with my belt," chimed in another man.

Ellie and I stood facing each other as hands started to guide us toward the exit. Sam came running through the dining car and flew up onto a table in front of us. Ellie reached out and took him into her arms.

"Clarence is on his way," he said. *"I found him locked in the mail room. One of your friends gave him a bump the size of a lemon on the back of his head."* Sam then looked around the dining car, noticing all the faces staring icy daggers at me. *"Nice going, kid. I see you're still making lots of friends. I leave you alone for two minutes and suddenly everybody on the train wants your hide."*

Not wanting to appear as if I had completely lost my mind, I whispered, "I can't help it. Nobody believes me about Connie and Ty, and *she* won't talk. Say something, Ellie! Tell them what happened!"

But for the first (and, I'm certain, the *only*) time in her life, Ellie Strasbourg was literally speechless. She opened her mouth, and moved her lips, but only a faint, pathetic squeak came out.

"What's the matter with her?" someone asked.

"That cat's got her tongue," someone answered. "They can do that, you know. They'll steal your breath as soon as they look at you. My great-aunt Betty's second cousin's daughter had a cat that killed a baby that way. You could look it up. It was in all the papers."

"Oh, for Pete's sake," said Sam. "Have we gone through some kind of railroad tunnel to the twelfth century? What's next—are they going to call me a witch and burn me at the stake?"

As the crowd of angry faces closed in tighter and tighter, I could practically feel the flames lapping up at me.

"Hold it right there, everyone! Nobody move!" shouted Clarence, storming in just in the nick of time. Something about the sound of his voice told the crowd that he was in no mood for foolishness, and everyone stopped dead in their tracks.

"Oh boy. I've never seen him this mad," said Sam.

"Now see here!" bellowed Judge Ambrose. "Who do you think—"

"Quiet!" said Clarence, grimacing as he rubbed the back of his head. "This is *my* train. Somebody tell me what is going on."

"Look!" I said, using the handcuffs to pull Ellie into his line of vision. "I've got her!"

Clarence's face brightened and broke into a huge smile. "Well, I'll be! Ellie! I can't tell you how good it is to see you! Are you okay? They didn't hurt you? Where . . . ?

How . . . ? We've got to get you back to your . . . Why are you two hand—"

The train whistle sounded again as we rumbled through the darkness and rain, closer and closer to the station in Ripley.

I didn't let him finish his question. "You have to hurry! Nobody believes me, but it was the Perfiddles! They're not who you think they are, *honest*. They're criminals! He's not a preacher, and she's definitely not going to have a baby. Their names are Connie and Ty, and they took Ellie, and then when I found her, they locked me up with her. They're going to get off at the next stop. And *he* has the Blue Streak! It's in his coat pocket. I saw him put it there."

Uncertainty rippled through the crowd.

"Connie and Ty?"

"Bank robbers!"

"On the FBI's most-wanted list, I've heard."

"They killed a man in Pittsburgh."

"Utterly preposterous," said Judge Ambrose, silencing the crowd with a wave of his platter-sized hand. "Mr. Nockwood, maybe that knock on the head wiped away the memory, but perhaps I can clear it up: you *watched* me put the necklace in the mailbag. And so did a number of other witnesses. Now, I'm a big enough man to admit that

I'm, uh . . . well, it appears I have *misjudged* this boy. Perhaps we should be praising him for finding the girl. But he's wrong about the Perfiddles and the necklace. Dead wrong. I'd stake my reputation on it."

"Listen to me, Clarence," said Sam, risking injury by moving to a spot between Clarence and the judge. *"Captain Hindenburg here isn't the only one to underestimate the kid. I was wrong, too. The fact is, the kid's been right about everything, from the very beginning. And he's right about who they are. Don't feel bad; they had everybody fooled. And if the kid says Ty has the necklace, I believe him."*

Clarence's eyes went from Sam to me, and then to Connie and Ty, before returning to the judge. "You're right, Judge. I saw you put *something* in the mailbag. But now that I think about it, Mrs. Strasbourg first handed the necklace to Reverend Perfiddle, who gave it to you. And do you remember what happened in those few seconds it was in his possession? He had a sneezing fit, and his lap and face were covered for a long time with that huge handkerchief of his. He must have used that time to make a switch. He put a fake necklace in the bag—just in case somebody checked—and pocketed the real one."

Ty stood, smiling broadly as he removed his coat and handed it to Clarence. "Please. Be my guest."

Clarence turned all the pockets inside out and patted the jacket thoroughly. No necklace. It was the Poughkeepsie Pickpocket all over again.

Ty smiled slyly, and Judge Ambrose humphed.

"That doesn't mean anything," I said. "Maybe he gave it to *her*."

"I've heard enough," said the judge. "It's time we got the girl back to her mother."

The words had barely left his mouth when Mrs. Strasbourg cried out Ellie's name. She came running into the car from her suite at the back of the train.

"My baby! Oh, thank you, thank you, thank you," she said to Judge Ambrose, as if *he* had anything to do with Ellie's safe return.

My mother, meanwhile, suddenly appeared from our humble section in the front of the train, carrying my baby sister and looking concerned. When she finally spotted me in the middle of all those strange, angry-looking people and handcuffed to Ellie, her look turned to one of absolute bewilderment.

"Henry?" She fought her way through the crowd. "You scared me to death. I woke up and you were gone. What is going on?"

"It's a long story," I said. "I've been . . . busy, I guess." I held up my handcuffed wrist, pulling Ellie's arm up with it.

At that moment, Ellie was looking over her mother's shoulders at Connie and Ty, who were starting to make their move toward the exit, one step behind Phyllis Finkleman and that little bit of Amazonian jungle living on top of her head.

Sam leaped up onto the table right in front of us and stood on his hind legs, with his front paws on Ellie's shoulders. As he looked deeply into her eyes, something strange began to happen: Sam's eyes began to glow—a soft, mossy green light at first, gradually turning brighter and brighter, until I could have sworn there were two enormous lightning bugs sticking out of his skull. At first, I was sure that it was pure coincidence: a trick of the light, a mere reflection. But Sam's face was in shadow; the light, I realized, was coming from his eyes.

Ellie, meanwhile, looked as if she were in a trance. In a matter of seconds, the skin of her hand and wrist, where she was handcuffed to me, turned ice-cold, and her eyes stared unblinkingly into Sam's.

"Listen to me, Ellie," said Sam in a voice that sounded different from the one I was used to—a little louder, a little clearer. *"If you can hear me, right now would be an excellent time to speak up. It's up to you, but if you don't say anything, those two crooks are going to get away with it."*

Ellie's eyes grew to the size of dinner plates, and finally, she blinked, breaking the spell. "I—I heard him!" she stammered. "Henry! I heard him! It's like he was inside my head."

"What is she talking about?" Judge Ambrose asked. "*Who* did she hear?"

I nudged Sam. "How did you do that? What happened to your eyes?"

"Shhh! Just watch and listen. It's going to get interesting." He climbed onto Clarence's shoulder to have a clear view.

Ellie stood up straight and pointed directly at Connie and Ty, who were still fighting their way through the crowd. "Stop them! Henry is telling the truth! They did it—Connie and Ty. They knocked me out, and kidnapped me, and then tied me up and gagged me in one of the compartments."

Connie and Ty stopped dead in their tracks, the path to the exit blocked by the suddenly boisterous crowd.

"And stop the lady in the funny hat!" she shouted over the noise.

"What? Why?" I asked. "Is she in on this with them?"

Ellie didn't answer, refusing to take her eyes off the silly stuffed goldfinches perched on Phyllis Finkleman's head.

In a flash Ty reached out to grab the hat, sending a few feathers flying toward the floor, but Phyllis saw him coming and ducked out of the way just in time.

"You keep your filthy hands away from me, you cheap crook," she said. "What did you do to my hat?" Her eyes never left Ty as she backed her way across the room to Ellie.

Then, as everyone in the car watched, Ellie reached up with her free hand and felt around in the bird's nest in the center of Phyllis's hat. Grinning triumphantly, she raised her hand from the nest and turned it over so that everyone could see what it held: her mother's extravagant necklace, with the world-famous Blue Streak sapphire dangling gloriously and sparkling like there was no tomorrow.

"Now *that's* what I call a nest egg," said Phyllis, shaking her head in disbelief.

I turned to Sam. "The hat? How did you know?"

He winked at me. *"Lucky guess."*

Don't Call Me Samantha
THE ALMOST ENTIRELY TRUE
AUTOBIOGRAPHY OF LANTERN SAM

And Then There Was One

The new name stuck. I wasn't just plain old Sam anymore; in the blink of an eye, I had become Lantern Sam. Which was fine by me, even if the way I had acquired the name wasn't anything to be proud of.

"Call me whatever you want," I told Clarence. "Just don't call me late for dinner, especially if there are sardines involved."

Frankly, I was more concerned about the fur on my belly, or, to be more accurate, the *lack* of fur on my belly. The railroad lantern had burned it so badly that it all fell out, leaving me with a bald patch that took months to grow back.

In the meantime, my life aboard the Shoreliner grew more interesting over the next few years. I developed my talent for sniffing out con men, crooks, and cads of every flavor, and managed to do it without risking any more of my precious lives. Two weeks to the day after Clarence and I had toasted my success in the Case of the Syracuse Swindler with a bottle of fresh Jersey milk, I noticed a familiar face pretending to guzzle gin in the lounge. Clarence called him Poughkeepsie Pete, and he was just about the slipperiest, sneakiest pickpocket this side of the Susquehanna. Once a month or so, he'd board in Poughkeepsie, and by the time we got to Schenectady, he had helped himself to the contents of any number of passengers' pockets.

But like I said, he was slippery. We were never able to catch him in the act, and on the three occasions that Clarence accused him of pocket picking, Pete calmly turned all of his own pockets inside out and invited Clarence, or anyone else, to search him. He was clean.

"There's only one possible answer," I said after it had happened the third time. "Pete has a partner in crime. I'll bet the stuff never even makes it to the bottom of his own pockets. He's handing it off before the dumb pigeons even know they've been robbed."

"But he boards alone," said Clarence. "And he's alone when he steps off. I've seen him, lots of times."

"Perhaps, but my thought is that he knows you're watching. He and his partner could get on at different ends of the platform, or even at different stations. If I had to guess, I'd bet it's a woman."

"Why a woman?"

"Because we're less likely to suspect a woman, silly."

"So, what do we do?"

"*We* don't do anything. You're going to go on doing whatever it is that you do, and I'm going to keep an eye on our old friend Poughkeepsie Pete."

"Getting a bit full of yourself, aren't you?" said Clarence. "What a cat! Solves a couple of crimes and now instead of Lantern Sam, he thinks he's Sam Spade himself."

He was right. Success was definitely going to my head. But it's not like I was living in the lap of luxury. I was sharing a cot in the dormitory car with Clarence, and I sometimes went *days* without a decent bowl of cream and *weeks* without a few measly sardines. So as far as I was concerned, I had earned the right to be a little arrogant.

That evening, as the Shoreliner rumbled west, I settled into my perch above the seats in the lounge for a little observing. Clarence had followed my directions perfectly, placing a folded blanket on top of the divider between the barbershop and the lounge, Pete's favorite hunting ground. From that vantage point, directly behind the bar and above the crowd, I had an unobstructed view of all the action.

I didn't have to wait for long. At eight-fifteen, Pete strolled in looking as if he owned the joint. He stood at one end of the bar and immediately struck up a conversation with a red-faced salesman. While he talked, though, his eyes were in constant motion, checking out every person in the room.

"Tell you what, Pete. You seem like a nice fella. Let me buy you a drink," said the salesman.

"No, no, I couldn't," said Pete. "This round is on me."

And then I watched something truly amazing. First, Pete motioned to the salesman to look at a pretty girl who had just come into the room. When the poor guy turned his head, Pete reached over and lifted the wallet from the inside pocket of his jacket. He got the bartender's attention, bought two drinks, and then dropped the wallet back in the salesman's pocket!

"Cheers!" said Pete, clinking glasses with his new "friend."

"Thanks, pal. Next one's on me, though."

Pete smiled as he moved on to his next victim. "If you insist."

He slid to the other end of the bar, where I watched him "borrow" someone's fountain pen to write something on the back of a business card. When he finished, he took a close look at the pen, chuckled, and said, "Junk," under his breath, and then returned it to its owner. I have to be honest: I was starting to respect Pete. Unlike most crooks, the guy had some standards.

After that he sat at the bar for a while, yawning and looking so bored that I thought he was about to give up for the night. That would have been fine by me; I was ready for a nap. Suddenly, though, he sat up straight on his stool. In the mirror, he had spotted the Grayfields, an elegantly dressed couple in their late sixties who, according to the newspapers, had recently donated a million dollars to a hospital in New York. He sprang to his feet, offering his seat to Mrs. Grayfield, who graciously accepted, and then he *really* turned on the charm. He bought them drinks (using his own money, even!) and before long, they were all roaring with laughter at a story he told them about the time he went swimming in May in the icy waters off Nantucket—where the Grayfields, as everyone also knew, just *happened* to own a summer home.

At the mention of Nantucket, a blond woman—a real hot tamale, by the way—who had been standing nearby, shrieked and then hurried over uninvited to join their conversation. "I apologize for eavesdropping, but I can't help myself. I just *love* Nantucket. In fact, I bought this hat there. Isn't it wonderful?"

I'm no expert on hats, but trust me, it *wasn't* wonderful, and if that jumble of ruffles and ribbons had ever been within a hundred miles of Nantucket, I'm the King of Siam.

The woman in the hat was so doggone chipper that the Grayfields couldn't help smiling politely as she yammered on and on and on, even though I'm quite sure that they wished they could disappear. From my perch, all I wanted was to knock the phony smile off her face and that even phonier hat off the top of her head.

And that's when it hit me. The hat! I'd seen it before; I was sure of it! The girl was different (or maybe she dyed her hair), but the hat was definitely the same one I had seen a few weeks earlier in the same car, not five feet from Poughkeepsie Pete.

After that, everything changed. Once I knew what I was looking for, I watched, fascinated, as Mr. Grayfield's pocket watch, cuff links, fountain pen, and a money clip holding a substantial wad of cash all found their way into the bottomless pit of that horrible hat. While one hand distracted Mr. Grayfield with a friendly pat on the back, or pretended to brush lint off his jacket, the long, thin fingers of the other crept into every pocket they could find and removed the contents with astonishing ease. Then, in a perfectly choreographed dance, the tamale would come closer to Pete, and all the goodies went into the hat. Sure, Pete was a crook, but watching him reminded me of the time I saw Vladimir Horowitz play the piano at Carnegie Hall, his fingers flying up and down the keyboard in a frenzy. Like Horowitz, Poughkeepsie Pete was a genius.

Of course, that didn't stop me from wanting to see him

and his pretty sidekick behind bars. A crook is a crook, and I had my own reputation to worry about. And so, when Miss Tamale started to make noises about going back to her room, I knew it was time for me to make my move.

I coiled myself like a spring and pounced, scattering that bonnet and Mr. Grayfield's possessions from one end of the car to the other. The tamale screamed as everyone else in the car froze, staring openmouthed at her.

"I . . . I . . . how did all that stuff get in there?" she asked.

"A very good question," said Clarence, who had walked in just in time to witness my flight and perfect landing. "I would love to hear your explanation. Come with me, miss. And you, too," he added with a look in Pete's direction.

"Me? What did I do?" Pete asked, his palms turned to the ceiling.

"Perhaps nothing," Clarence said. "But let's find out for sure." He led them away to the mail room, where he locked them up until we got to the next station.

I wasn't in the room for that interrogation, but Clarence told me later that the girl spilled her guts immediately. Pete admitted to nothing, uttering just five words: "I'm gonna kill that cat."

When we arrived in Cleveland, the police were waiting at the station to take custody of Poughkeepsie Pete and Miss Tamale, but Pete had one final parting gift for me. The

Shoreliner's engineer traveled with his dog, a behemoth named Peaches who was known far and wide for his hatred of all cats. I quickly learned to stay on the train while we were in the station in Cleveland, because the engineer would let Peaches out for a quick run outside before departing. I did not have a plan, however, if Peaches decided to come into the dormitory car, where I was minding my own business and trying to catch up on some much-deserved sleep.

As the police slapped the handcuffs on Pete and led him onto the platform, he shouted, "Come here, boy! Get the kitty!"

Every hair on my body stood on end, and in a flash, Peaches roared through the car like a tornado, twisting and howling as he sought me out. I bolted to the other end of the car, out the door, and into the maze of tracks, switches, and slow-moving trains, some arriving, some departing. Glancing over my shoulder, I saw Peaches burst through the open door after me, so I took a chance and ran between the wheels of a moving boxcar, hoping that he wouldn't be foolish enough to follow. As I came out the other side, I found myself in the middle of another set of tracks with an accelerating locomotive bearing down on me from one direction and Peaches, who was even more persistent than I thought, galloping toward me from the other. I hesitated for a split second, then leaped to the far side of the tracks, away from Peaches.

For a few moments, we stared at each other through the wheels of the train as it *clackety-clacked* its way out of the rail yard. Lucky for me, it was a long train; I had time to catch my breath before figuring out how to get back aboard the Shoreliner and not get left behind. I was pretty sure that the engineer wouldn't leave without Peaches, so all I had to do was get back before him.

I waited about one second too long. The section of rail that I was leaning against shifted suddenly, and before I knew what was happening, my tail felt as if it were being squeezed in a vise. I couldn't move; I was trapped in the switching mechanism that makes it possible for trains to move from one set of tracks to another.

Peaches, meanwhile, paced back and forth on the other side of the moving train, whose caboose was getting closer and closer. As if that situation wasn't quite bad enough, in the rail yard behind me, the engineer of yet *another* train sounded its horn, warning me to get off his track.

It didn't look good for ol' Lantern Sam. Heaven knows I've had my share of close calls and near misses (along with, let's face it, a few direct hits), but it looked like my luck had finally run out. The only thing left to the Fates to decide was whether Peaches or the 5:15 from Akron would reach me first.

Heading in opposite directions, the two trains rumbled on

for an eternity, it seemed. Finally, the caboose of the departing train went by, its wheels squeaking noisily. With no train
between us, Peaches threw himself into action, sending dirt
and gravel flying in all directions as his giant paws tore into
the ground.

Behind me, the 5:15 from Akron drew closer, horn blar-
ing and brakes squealing. Fifteen feet . . . ten feet . . . five
feet . . .

Peaches covered the short distance in no time, lunging at
me with teeth bared and a look on his face that would have
scared his own mother.

I squeezed my eyes shut and waited.

And then, nothing.

No Peaches tearing me limb from limb. No 5:15 from
Akron squashing me like an insect.

I was still alive, and not only that, my tail was free again.
At the crucial moment, the switch had opened, sending the
train hurtling harmlessly past me and directly into the path of
Peaches. Lucky for him, the cowcatcher did its job and tossed
him to the side of the tracks without a scratch. He would live
to fight another day.

And once again, we found ourselves on opposite sides of
a moving train. This time, though, I was on the side closest to
the Shoreliner, and I hightailed it back to the dormitory car.
(Technically, I suppose I *bent*-tailed it. The top four inches of

my tail were permanently kinked, with the tip pointing to the left.)

Clarence was waiting for me. "Where have you been? I was starting to worry that you wouldn't make it back in time."

"Just out getting a little fresh air and exercise," I said.

"What's wrong with your tail? Somebody slam a door on it?"

"Something like that."

"Well, be careful. I know you cats have nine lives and all, but that's no excuse for carelessness. After that little incident with the lantern, I think you're down to eight."

I didn't have the heart to tell him that, by my count, he was off by seven.

Chapter 9

"I'll take that, if you don't mind," said Ty calmly, his revolver pointed right at Ellie's heart.

Women screamed. Men rushed forward, stopping when Ty waved the gun in their faces.

"Don't nobody do nothing stupid," he said, sneering. "Just stay where you are, everybody. I ain't afraid to use Roscoe here." He turned the gun back to Ellie and held out his other hand. "Hand over the necklace, little lady, and nobody gets hurt."

Ellie narrowed her eyes and stuck her chin out. "Maybe I will and maybe I won't."

"Oh, I think you will," said Connie, pulling her own gun and pointing it at Mrs. Strasbourg. "Tell your little princess to drop the rocks."

The next thirty seconds lasted an eternity, and to this day, seventy-five years later, the events still play in extra-slow motion in my dreams, exactly the way I remember it all happening.

"Give him the necklace, Ellie," said Clarence in a calm voice. "You heard what she said. They're just *rocks*. Not worth anybody getting hurt over."

Mrs. Strasbourg smiled at her. "He's right, sweetheart. They don't mean a thing."

Ellie looked at Sam, still sitting up straight on Clarence's shoulder. He nodded at her, and I looked around the room to see if anyone else had seen him do it. I guess no one expects a kid to be asking a cat for advice, though, because nobody seemed to notice anything out of the ordinary.

"Get ready, Henry," said Sam. *"There's an emergency brake cord right behind you—do you see it? Good. When I give the signal, I want you to grab that cord and pull with everything you've got."*

"Are you sure?" I whispered. "What if—"

"Clarence, tell him it's okay," said Sam. The sound of the train under our feet changed pitch as we started across a trestle bridge, high over Chautauqua Creek.

Clarence scratched his head, took a deep breath, and nodded. "Okay. I'm going to trust you, Sam. Do what he says, Henry."

Ty moved a step closer to Ellie, his gun still trained on her. "C'mon, kid. Time's up."

"Get ready, Henry," said Sam. *"Remember, pull like your life depends on it. Because it does."*

I edged back to the side of the car and felt around until I found the emergency brake cord.

Ellie's hand—the one not handcuffed to me, that is—remained tightly wrapped around the Blue Streak. "You're going to jail, mister. And so are you," she added with a sneer in Connie's direction. "And *I'm* going to help put you there. Here—take it."

She held the necklace out to Ty, who rudely snatched it from her fingers and then held it up to the light to admire it. For a few precious seconds, he was spellbound—utterly *hypnotized*—by the dazzling blue sapphire. That moment of hesitation would cost him dearly.

From his perch on Clarence's shoulder, Sam shouted at me, *"NOW, Henry!"*

I held my breath and pulled with all my might. Sam, meanwhile, launched himself toward Ty, a good six or eight feet away. The image of that calico missile flying through the air with all seventeen claws extended and teeth bared while screaming *"Mrrrraaaaa!"* is one that no one in that dining car will ever forget. Nor are they likely to forget the look on Ty's face, or his girlish, high-pitched scream as the majority of those skillfully sharpened claws dug into the skin of his neck and back.

As the train's brakes took hold, screeching and squealing (*almost* as loud as Ty), everyone lurched forward, and a stumbling, sliding, careening, cursing mob hurtled toward the front of the car—with Sam and Ty leading the way. In desperation, Connie reached out and grabbed Ellie, dragging her to the floor, and suddenly I found myself clinging to the brake cord with one hand as the steel of the handcuffs cut deeper and deeper into the wrist that was still bound to Ellie.

Everything changed in a hurry, though. As I held on for dear life, I felt a distinct "snap" inside my wrist where the cuff pressed against it, and I almost passed out from the lightning bolt of pain that shot up my arm. The next thing I knew, the three of us—Connie, Ellie, and me—were crashing into Ty, who was still screaming and thrashing about, bleeding profusely and trying to rid himself of the crazed calico fly-papered to his face.

Over the eardrum-shattering noise of the wheels, screeching and skidding along the iron rails, and through the waves of pain in my arm, I heard one final, hideous scream from Ty as Sam bit into the soft, fleshy part of his hand—the one holding the Blue Streak. The necklace hit the floor and slid away from them, coming to rest against the doorframe at the front of the car.

Connie, seeing the necklace slipping away, let go of Ellie (and her gun) and dived after it. Her revolver slid across the floor, stopping momentarily next to the necklace and then continuing into the vestibule. The sudden, violent braking had slammed open the train's exit doors, and the gun skittered against the wall, spinning like a top for a moment before clanking down the steps and out of the train.

And still the train kept on, skidding on and on down the tracks; stopping several hundred tons of speeding iron isn't like stopping Grandpa's Ford, I learned.

Seeing the gun go overboard made Connie more determined to save the necklace, and her hand swung out to grab the jewels, missing by mere inches as they shook loose from their resting spot and started to slide toward the open door.

Making one last, desperate attempt to prevent the Blue Streak from falling onto the tracks, Ty somersaulted past his partner in crime, losing his grip and flying into the vestibule. He screamed as he bounced off the doorframe and slid feetfirst out the right side door, stopping himself from falling out of the train only at the last possible second, when he managed to reach up and grab hold of the hand-rail at the bottom step.

While his feet and legs dangled over the side, he begged for help, his cries becoming more and more desperate-sounding.

Not surprisingly, Connie's eyes remained on the prize. She ignored Ty's pleading, pouncing instead in the direction of the Blue Streak. But Sam, Ellie, and I caught her in mid-pounce and wrestled her back to the floor before she could grab it. In the midst of that struggle, however, Connie landed a direct hit with her foot, sending Sam flying into the vestibule. Sam hit the floor with all four feet running, but it made no difference; his claws were useless on the hard, cold steel floor, like worn tires spinning in the snow. His eyes met mine, and in the middle of the confusion and squealing and screeching, I heard two words: "Judge . . . father . . ."

And then, along with everyone else in that dining car, I watched in horror as Lantern Sam and the Blue Streak flew out the left side door of the Lake Erie Shoreliner and into the coal-black night.

"SAM!" cried Clarence and Ellie.

"Noooo!" screamed Connie, watching her dreams of riches disappear.

I remember opening my mouth and trying to scream Sam's name, but it was my turn to be speechless.

After an eternity, the Shoreliner came to a stop. Clarence ran past me into the vestibule, stopping abruptly when he looked out the open door.

"Oh no," he said quietly.

"He'll be all right, won't he?" I asked. After all, I reasoned, we weren't going that fast when he was thrown from the train, and everyone knows that cats always land on their feet. However, Clarence's face when he looked out the door did not exactly give me hope that I was right. "What is it? What's the matter?"

A sad smile curled his lips, and he shook his head, ever so slightly. "We're in the middle of the bridge over the Chautauqua Creek Gorge. I grew up just a few miles from here. . . . I know the spot like the back of my hand. It's got to be two hundred feet—straight down. Nothing but creek. And rocks."

"Wh-what?" asked Ellie, her eyes filling with tears. "It can't be. It just can't."

I blinked back a tear or two of my own as I glanced down into the deep valley below us. "Sam," I whispered into the blackness.

Clarence took out his handkerchief, wiped his brow, and then turned on his heels, where he saw the bloodied, beaten, and helpless Ty hanging from the handrail, trying (and failing) to pull himself back into the train.

"Somebody . . . help . . . me," groaned Ty. "Can't . . . hold . . . much . . . longer . . ."

"Give me a hand up here," said Clarence, who was quickly joined by two men who were picking themselves up from the dining car floor. Together, they yanked Ty into the safety of the car, where he crumpled under his own weight.

In the excitement of the moment, I had forgotten about my broken wrist—that is, until Ellie decided to pull me toward our mothers.

"Owwwww!" I yelled.

Ellie started to ask, "What's the matt—" but she stopped when she saw my arm.

When I saw the funny look on her face, I gathered my courage and glanced down at my handcuffed wrist . . . and my knees turned wobbly and my head suddenly felt very light. My hand hung at a very unnatural angle and had already turned several shocking shades of purple and yellow.

"Henry!" cried my mother. "What's wrong?"

"He's got a broken wrist," said Clarence. "We've got to get those handcuffs off before they cut off his circulation completely and he loses his hand."

"Ty," I whispered hoarsely. I was getting dizzier and dizzier by the second. "He must have the key."

"You don't look so good," said Ellie, righting an overturned chair. "You'd better sit down for a while."

Behind us, Gladys and Gwendolyn dragged "Mrs. Perfiddle" to her feet, and there was nothing gentle about it. My vision was a little fuzzy, but I was able to make out the gun in Gwendolyn's hand, which she kept pointed at Connie.

"I'm not afraid to use this," Gwendolyn warned Connie. "Our daddy taught us how to use guns back on the farm in Indiana. You try anything, you'll find out how good a shot I am."

Phyllis Finkleman cackled, pointing at the pillow sticking out from between the buttons of Connie's coat. "Well, will you look at that! The boy was telling the truth—she's no more *pregnant* than I am!"

"So it would seem," said Judge Ambrose. "And now, Miss Henshaw, maybe it's best if you give that pistol to me."

Gwendolyn handed it to him, a bit reluctantly, I thought.

"Boys, get something to tie them up with," said the judge. "I'll turn them over to the local authorities in Erie."

"I've got a better idea," said Clarence, holding up the ring full of keys that he'd taken from Ty's pocket. "I know where there's a perfectly good set of handcuffs."

"Shame about your, uh, cat," Judge Ambrose said to Clarence after Ellie and I were finally separated and Connie and Ty were cuffed together. "Never cared much for cats myself, but he seemed like a good—"

Clarence stared at him, expressionless. "*Don't.* Just get yourself and those two . . . miserable excuses for human beings off my train. And next time, do us all a favor and take the Twentieth Century Limited." He turned and walked away, helping passengers to their feet and reassuring everyone that the danger was over. "We'll be under way in a minute," he added, checking his pocket watch. "Good thing we were a little ahead of schedule."

Julia, the Strasbourgs' maid, used some clean towels from the kitchen to wrap my arm until I could see a doctor for a proper plaster cast.

"How does that feel?" she asked when she had finished. "Not too tight, is it?"

"No, it's okay," I said, closing my eyes and trying to ignore the dull, aching pain. In the background, Mrs. Strasbourg and my mother chatted with Clarence, who did his best to explain how two kids had gone from being complete strangers to being handcuffed together in the compartment of two of the FBI's most-wanted criminals. Of course, he left out Sam's part in the whole story. Maybe he didn't think they'd believe him, or maybe he just wasn't ready to talk about Sam yet.

Ellie, sitting beside me on one of the benches in the dining car, leaned over and whispered in my ear, "I really did hear him."

"I know," I said, not opening my eyes.

"It's funny; I remember him looking at me, and I remember that there was something . . . funny about his eyes, but I can't remember what it was," she said. "It's like that memory was just *erased*. You don't suppose that Sam . . ."

I sat up suddenly, my eyes wide open. "He said something else, right before he . . . There was so much noise that I couldn't hear it all, but I caught two words: *judge* and *father*. Did you hear it?"

Ellie shook her head. "Maybe Clarence did, though."

"Good idea. What was he trying to tell us about Judge Ambrose?"

At the front of the car, the judge chomped on a fresh cigar as he sniffed around the vestibule, where Sam and the Blue Streak had last been seen.

"What is he doing up there?" Ellie whispered.

"I think he's still looking for your mom's necklace," I said.

"But it went out the door with . . . I mean, I didn't imagine that, did I? It fell into the gorge."

"I guess he's just making sure."

Ahead of us, the engineer sounded the whistle, and the train jerked into motion. I peered out the window into the emptiness around us and imagined for a moment that we were flying across the valley.

"Poor Sam," I said.

"Poor Clarence," said Ellie.

We sat quietly for a few seconds, our minds full of the past few hours' adventures.

Ellie nudged me with her elbow. "I haven't thanked you properly for rescuing me."

"I didn't really *rescue* you. They were just going to leave you tied up in that room until somebody found you."

"But you didn't give up," she said. "You were like one of King Arthur's knights. You're a *hero*."

"I'm not a *hero*," I protested, blushing furiously. "It was Sam who—"

I looked up to find our mothers standing over us, smiling. "Hey, kids," said Mrs. Strasbourg. "We have some exciting news. You need to get ready—we're *all* getting off the train at Erie."

"W-we are?" I asked. "Why? What about Father? His ship will be coming in. We have to be there."

Mrs. Strasbourg smiled. "Don't worry about that—we'll see that your father joins us in Erie. You're all going to be our guests for a few days. First things first, though. We have to get you to a doctor and have that arm looked after properly. Then you'll be spending the day at Conneaut Lake Park, where you will be riding the Blue Streak as many times as you like. How does that sound?"

"But . . . how will we get back to Ashtabula?" I asked.

Ellie's mom laughed. "Your mother was right. You *are* a worrier! Young man, after all you've done for my family, believe me, I'll give you a ride home—or anywhere else you want to go."

"Yay!" cried Ellie. "We're going to ride the Blue Streak a hundred times!"

A porter came through the car, announcing, "Next stop, Ripley, New York! Ripley next!"

"We have to hurry," Mother said. "Erie is the next stop after Ripley. Doris, thank you so much—we'll meet you on the platform." The Strasbourgs headed for their suite at the back of the train, while we went forward to our section to get our bags.

"See you in a few minutes!" said Ellie.

I searched frantically for Clarence as the train slowed to a stop at the Erie station, and ran up and down the platform looking for him. After everything that had happened—especially Sam's accident—I couldn't get off the Shoreliner without talking to him. Finally, I spotted him helping Madeline Parker and Alabama Woodward with their numerous bags.

"That's strange," I thought. "Why are they getting off in Erie? Shouldn't they be continuing on to Chicago?"

"Clarence!" I shouted, tripping over my own feet and nearly falling as I ran to him. As I glanced up into his eyes, I thought he looked older than he had at the beginning of our journey.

"Easy there, Henry," he said. "One broken limb at a time."

"I've been looking everywhere for you. Ellie's family invited us to their house, so we're getting off here instead of Ashtabula, and I was afraid I would never see you again. I just wanted to say . . . I'm really sorry about Lantern Sam. He was the best cat . . . ever. And to say . . ." My voice drifted off; I wasn't exactly sure what I wanted to say, but I knew enough about life to know that *something* needed to be said.

Clarence took my hand, squeezing and shaking it firmly and looking deep into my eyes. "It's been my pleasure, Mr. Shipley. I'm proud of you, my boy—what you did back there . . . not a lot of adults could have done it. I want you to keep in touch. I want to hear more about that ship of your father's. Can you do that for me?"

Judge Ambrose stepped off the train and waited for Connie and Ty, joined at the ankles with their own handcuffs. I couldn't help smiling to myself as they stumbled across the platform, bickering and cursing at one another.

"Stop stepping on my feet, you moron," said Connie.

"Maybe if your feet weren't so big, I wouldn't keep doing it," answered Ty.

"Maybe if your IQ was bigger than my shoe size, you might actually learn to walk properly."

"And they lived happily ever after," said Clarence, watching Judge Ambrose lead them into the station. "Thanks to you, we've all seen the last of those two for a long, long time."

"I hope it's the last I see of all *three* of them," I said.

"I agree." He checked his pocket watch, as I'd seen him do a dozen times since New York City. "Three minutes behind schedule. Tsk, tsk. Maybe we can make it up west of Cleveland. Now remember what I said—I want to hear from you, Henry."

"Yes, sir. I'll do it. I'll send you a picture of the *Point Pelee*."

"That would be very nice. I'll look forward to it. Now go on . . . and take care of your mother and your little sister, you hear?"

"I will; I promise. Before I go, I have one more question:

back when Sam was . . . well, right before he . . . did you hear him say anything? Because I thought I heard him say . . ."

"Something about the judge . . . and Connie? I didn't catch the rest of it. Sorry, but I really have to get going, Henry. You take care of that wrist, okay?" He hurried to the train, stepping aboard just as it started to pull away from the platform.

Mother and Jessica were waiting for me near the entrance to the station, and I began to walk toward them.

"Henry! Hurry!" cried a voice behind me. I turned around to see Clarence waving madly and motioning to me to run as the Shoreliner slowly picked up speed.

As I ran along the edge of the platform, Clarence leaned out of the open door to talk to me. "Something Judge Ambrose said doesn't fit," he said. "The knock I got on my head when they locked me in the mail room—remember, the judge mentioned it. He *knew* what had happened. But Sam's the only one I told."

I was running out of platform. "I don't understand," I shouted as the train, and Clarence, slipped away into the darkness.

Chapter 10

Inside the train station at Erie, Judge Ambrose and Mrs. Strasbourg talked to a deputy from the local sheriff's office, who then led Connie and Ty out to his car and drove them away. Another deputy stayed behind to interview Ellie and me, but after only a couple of questions, Mrs. Strasbourg put her foot down.

"It's just going to have to wait until tomorrow," she said. "My daughter has been through a very traumatic experience, and she needs to sleep. And this young man—the one who saved my daughter's life—has a broken wrist and must be in absolute agony. *You* are going to make yourself useful by driving him to the local hospital or the nearest doctor. I don't care if you have to wake somebody up—do whatever it takes to ensure that he gets the best possible care. You do have an automobile, don't you?"

"Yes, ma'am," he said, flustered at being told what to do by this no-nonsense woman. "Right this way." We followed him out into the parking area.

"Perfect," she said. "Henry, you ride with the officer. We'll follow you." She held up a white-gloved hand, and less than ten seconds later, a long black car pulled up to the curb and the driver hopped out.

"Evening, Mrs. Strasbourg," he said, tipping his cap. "Sorry to keep you waiting."

"Not at all, Billings. Your timing is perfect, as usual. We have some extra passengers. Our new friends, Mrs. Shipley and Jessica, will be joining us for a day or two."

Billings tipped his cap at Mother. "Glad to have you aboard, Mrs. Shipley. Make yourself comfortable. We'll be at the Conneaut Hotel in no time at all."

"Julia, do you mind riding up front with Billings? I don't think we'll all fit in the back."

"No, ma'am. I like it up there. He's teaching me how to drive."

"Not tonight, I hope," said Mrs. Strasbourg. "Billings, we'll be making a stop along the way. Follow that car."

It was nearly two o'clock in the morning when we left the hospital, and well after three when we pulled into the driveway at the Hotel Conneaut—a place I'd heard about all my life but had never seen. As the headlights of the Strasbourgs' car swung through the park, my heart raced when I caught a glimpse of the curving, skeletal spine of a massive sleeping dinosaur—actually, the towering wooden framework of the Blue Streak. When I closed my eyes, I imagined the wind whooshing through my hair and the sound of screaming riders as we plummeted from the summit at over sixty miles per hour! I quickly came back to reality as Billings pulled up to the door of the hotel and set the emergency brake, and we all stumbled sleepily from the car.

Mrs. Strasbourg led the way inside as two porters whisked my bag away before I had a chance to pick it up. Despite the lateness of the hour, the lobby bustled with activity.

"Welcome back to the Hotel Conneaut, Mrs. Strasbourg," said the clerk, a cheerful, pink-cheeked man. "Tomorrow's a very big day for us, but of course you know that already. Your rooms are ready—the presidential suite and one standard room—so I won't keep you. It's a good thing you called when you did. Not five minutes later, I had to turn away a nice young couple. I hated to do it—she's expecting a baby, and the poor thing looked exhausted. I felt like the innkeeper in Bethlehem!" He laughed at his own little joke; he was the only one who did. Then he leaned over the desk, lowering his voice. "But the real excitement happened about an hour ago. You'll never guess who checked in. Madeline Parker, that's who! She's even more beautiful in person. I thought I was going to *die*!"

"Goodness," said Mrs. Strasbourg, not nearly as impressed as the clerk had hoped she'd be. "Will she be at the Dreamland Ballroom for the gala tomorrow night?"

"She's going to *sing*," said the clerk, hopping up and down excitedly. "It's a dream come true for me."

"Yes, well, how nice for you. May we have our keys, please?"

"My gosh! Of course!" he exclaimed, taking the keys from the rack behind him and handing them to Mrs. Strasbourg and Mother. "Pleasant dreams!"

Lucky for us, the opening ceremony for the Blue Streak was scheduled for one o'clock in the afternoon. Even though my arm ached, and I conked myself in the head with the cast at least twice, I managed to sleep until after ten o'clock, the latest I had ever slept in. (Growing up with a ship's captain for a father meant following ship's watches, and the "forenoon" watch started at eight o'clock *sharp*.)

Mother, her hair and makeup done and wearing her

"second-best dress," was sitting beside my bed when I opened my eyes.

"How's my son the hero this morning?" she asked, gently touching my plaster-encased wrist.

"My arm hurts. It itches, too."

"Your father is going to be so proud of you. Not prouder than I am, though. Just promise me one thing: no more adventures, all right?"

"I . . . uh, sure. This cast is going to make it hard . . . for a while, at least."

"The doctor said you were lucky. It's a clean break. The cast will be off in six weeks."

"That's all of June," I said glumly. "And some of July. No baseball. No swimming. That stinks."

"Come on, lazybones," Mother teased. "Why don't you get yourself cleaned up and into some nice clothes, and then let's find you something to eat. You must be *starving*. Jessica and I will meet you downstairs in the lobby in a few minutes. It looks like a perfect day."

When she was gone, I climbed out of bed, stopping when my eyes landed on something that must have fallen from my pants pocket when I undressed the night before: the sardine can key.

Those final few seconds on the bridge came flooding back to me as I bent down to pick it up.

"Sam," I whispered, dropping into a chair next to the bed and squeezing the key between my fingers. Whatever appetite I'd had moments earlier was gone. It all just felt *wrong;* I was at Conneaut Lake Park for the grand opening of the fastest, scariest roller coaster in the whole world, but I couldn't enjoy it—not really, not the way I'd always imagined it.

In Mother's suitcase, I found the sewing kit that she took with her wherever she went, and I unrolled several inches of strong black thread, which I used to hang the sardine key around my neck. I stood in front of the mirror, admiring my work.

"I'll wear it forever," I swore to myself.

By the time I entered the dining room and found Mother and Mrs. Strasbourg finishing their coffees and Ellie looking bored, my appetite had returned. In a matter of seconds I demolished a plate heaped with eggs, bacon, potatoes, and toast, and downed two glasses of orange juice.

"Are you finished *yet*?" Ellie asked. "What is taking you so long? Don't you *want* to see the Blue Streak?"

"Slow down, Ellie," warned her mother. "Let the poor boy enjoy his breakfast. You'll have plenty of time to show him around before the big opening."

"Did I miss anything . . . about Connie and Ty?" I asked. "Are they in jail? Did anybody find the . . . your necklace . . . or . . . Sam?"

"Now that you mention it, no. We haven't heard anything yet," said Mrs. Strasbourg. "It must have been too late to make the morning newspaper, but I would have thought it would be all over the radio by now. Quite a feather in Judge Ambrose's cap, I'd think, bringing in those two. I have no doubt that he'll take all the credit. He'll probably run for governor."

"Governor! He didn't do anything!" I protested. "He didn't even believe me when I . . . he told everyone it was *me* who did it! If it was all up to him, they would have gotten away with it. It's his fault that your necklace . . . and Sam . . . are gone."

"Easy, honey," said Mother, patting down my cowlick. "The only important thing right now is that you and Ellie are both safe and those awful people are in jail."

"Your mother's right, Henry," said Mrs. Strasbourg. "Ellie, why don't you take Henry on a tour of the park. You can ride those—what do you call them?—crash cars."

"Dodge-ems!" cried Ellie. "Let's go! You're going to love them, Henry!"

Mrs. Strasbourg handed Ellie and me printed yellow

tickets. "Those are good for the whole day—you can ride anything you want, as much as you want."

I hesitated. It was too good to be true. "I . . . I . . . can I, really? Isn't Father . . ."

"Go!" Mother urged. "It's a beautiful day. We'll meet you for the ceremony at a quarter of one. Just be careful of your cast, all right?"

After more than an hour of bumping, spinning, and twirling on the Dodge-ems and the Tumble Bug, and marveling at the forest of lumber that supported the winding rails of the Blue Streak, we walked across the midway and bought candied apples.

"Are you ready to admit yet that I was right?" Ellie asked, smiling smugly despite the juice dripping down her chin.

"About what?"

"Remember yesterday afternoon, right after we first met Lantern Sam and Clarence? You said that once you got off the train, you would never see me again, and I told *you* that we were going to be friends forever, and then you laughed at me. Well, ha-ha back at you, because you got off the train with me and here we are."

"It's one day! It hasn't even been twenty-four hours.

That's not forever. What's going to happen after today? I'm going home, and you're going back to New York."

"You just can't admit that I'm right and you're wrong."

"The only thing I'll admit is that you're stubborn."

"I'm not stubborn. I'm *right*."

Across the midway, a flash of sunlight reflecting off a man's bald head caught my eye—it was Judge Ambrose! I would have known that rotund head and matching body anywhere. "What's *he* doing here?" I snarled.

"Who? Ohhh. *Him*."

"Come on; don't let him see us," I said, leading Ellie around a corner and out of sight. "I don't want to have to talk to him."

"Shouldn't he be in court or something?" she asked, peeking around the side of the building.

"It's Sunday," I said.

"So? Criminals don't take Sunday off. Judges shouldn't, either."

I grinned at her. "Maybe he's here to ride the Blue Streak, just like us."

"I find that *very* hard to believe. It's weird, isn't it? He's here. Madeline Parker and that Alabama man. Your family. My family. Half the people from the train are here. I wonder if there's anybody else."

"I'll bet you a nickel that Phyllis Finkleman is here."

"Who?"

"You know, that lady with the whole flock of birds on her head. She's some kind of gossip reporter, and I think she's following Madeline Parker and her husband. Except she doesn't know they're married. That's why she won't leave them alone. But if they're here, she's here."

"That's terrible," said Ellie.

"Look! There she is!" Sure enough, standing across the midway and pretending to read a newspaper was Phyllis, but instead of birds, a bouquet of mixed flowers seemed to have sprouted from the top of her head. It was obvious to me that she was spying on someone.

Following the direction of her gaze, I spotted Madeline Parker and Alabama Woodward, who were laughing and enjoying a huge puff of pink cotton candy.

"Maybe we ought to warn them," I said. "I would hate it if somebody was spying on me all the—" The clanging of a bell cut me off—it was time for the grand opening of the Blue Streak!

We ran all the way to the temporary platform that had been set up near the entrance. The stage was decked out in flags and banners; it looked as if it were ready for a Fourth of July celebration, and across the opening to the roller coaster was a wide bright blue ribbon. When we got close,

Ellie cried out, "That's Daddy!" and took off ahead of me, racing up the steps of the platform, where her father, fresh off an eastbound train from one of his shipbuilding yards in Cleveland, had joined her mother.

And that's when I got a surprise of my own: my father, looking slightly uncomfortable in a dark suit, waved to me from the platform.

"Henry!" he shouted. "Come on up!"

I stopped and stared for a moment; he smiled at me, then turned and whispered something in Mother's ear— something that made her laugh out loud.

"What are you waiting for?" said Father.

I flew up the stairs and into his arms, where he hugged me tight for a long time, then mussed my hair. He held me by the shoulders in front of him and looked me up and down, performing his usual home-from-the-sea inspection.

"You've grown an inch," he declared. "And you're too thin. We need to get some meat on those bones. And some proper trousers. Those don't really fit you anymore. And you need a haircut. You look like one of my crew!"

"Yes, sir."

"But it is good to see you, son. Your mother tells me you had quite a trip yesterday. I can't wait to hear all about it."

Ellie came toward us, holding tightly to her father's hand.

"Here he is, Daddy. This is Henry Shipley, the boy I was telling you about."

Mr. Strasbourg reached out his hand and I shook it firmly, the way Father taught me. "Well, Henry Shipley, it is a real pleasure to meet the boy who rescued my daughter. I don't know how I can ever repay you."

"I—I—it's nice to meet you, sir," I stammered, looking to my father for help.

"Mr. Strasbourg, I'm Charles Shipley. We've met before; I'm—"

"Captain of the *Point Pelee*," finished Mr. Strasbourg. "Of course I remember you. Good to see you again, Charles." He pointed to me with his chin. "That's a fine boy you've got, Shipley. Very fine, indeed."

"Thank you, sir. I'm proud of him."

Just then the bell rang again and I turned around to find that a crowd of several hundred people had gathered around the stage.

The master of ceremonies, looking quite ridiculous (at least I thought so) in an Uncle Sam suit with striped suspenders, a straw hat, and a red, white, and blue bow tie, came around to us and asked us to take our seats.

"Here? On the stage?" I asked.

Father winked at me. "Get used to it, son. You're a hero."

"What? No, I'm not. I didn't do anything special. Anybody could have done it."

"Maybe, maybe not," said Father. "But the way I understand it is, you actually *did* it."

"Ladies and gentlemen," cried the master of ceremonies, "boys and girls, welcome to Conneaut Lake Park for the grand opening of the most spectacular roller coaster in all of America, if not the world—the Blue Streak! Before we get on with the ribbon cutting and other festivities, I'd like to ask some special guests to join me here on the stage. Judge Ambrose? Are you out there?"

My eyes almost popped out of my head. Criminy, what was it going to take to get away from that guy?

"On my way," the judge shouted, pushing through the crowd. The stairs creaked noisily under his feet, and then there he was, brushing past my knees as he joined the emcee at the front of the stage.

"Here he is, ladies and gentlemen," said the man in the Uncle Sam suit. "A criminal's worst nightmare and Crawford County's most famous citizen: Judge J. P. Ambrose! You may think you know old 'Hanging Joe' Ambrose, but what you probably don't realize is that this man has a heart of *gold*. A few years back, in his hometown, he started the Linesville School for Wayward Children, giving troubled young people a second chance and a place to learn an honest trade. Today, two members of the class of 1932—the school's first graduating class—will join a very select group as the Blue Streak races around its track for the very first time. Please welcome Miss Sally Oatley and Mr. Thomas Stapleton!"

Sally and Thomas must have been somewhere behind the platform, because I didn't see them moving through the crowd. Suddenly they popped up onto the stage, where they were immediately surrounded by people eager to shake their hands, including Uncle Sam and Judge Ambrose.

Next to be introduced was Edward Vettel, the designer of the Blue Streak, followed by Mr. Strasbourg, who was, in turn, followed by a politician from Harrisburg who looked pained to be there—as if it were the last place on earth he wanted to be on a beautiful Sunday in May. He told everyone who would listen about the golf game he was missing.

The master of ceremonies cleared a space at the front of the stage before he made his final introduction: "And now please join me in welcoming our very special guest, the woman who will cut the ribbon, officially opening the Blue Streak for business. She's a star of stage and screen, and she will be giving a one-time-only performance in the park's famed Temple of Music tonight. . . . Ladies and gentlemen, Miss Madeline Parker!"

She had been waiting at the back of the stage and bounded out as the crowd greeted her enthusiastically. I looked down into the crowd, and sure enough, there was Phyllis Finkleman, in the front row, the flowers in her hat wobbling back and forth as she frantically scribbled notes on her pad.

"Thank you so much!" Madeline shouted, her powerful stage voice reaching even those in the very back. "Ed Vettel is an old friend, and I was thrilled that he asked me to be here at Conneaut Lake Park today for the unveiling of his latest and, he assures me, his greatest creation. I have a little announcement I'd like to make—well, maybe not so little," she added, smiling.

"Alabama, would you come here, please?"

Although he looked uncertain, Alabama joined her.

"Folks, I'd like to introduce someone to you—someone you're going to be hearing a lot about one day soon. This handsome gentleman is Mr. Alabama Woodward, and he is the finest playwright on Broadway. I'm also very proud to tell you that he happens to be—as of yesterday—my husband!"

They may not have known who he was, and they certainly had not seen any of his plays, but the people in the crowd knew a big story when they heard it, and they cheered wildly.

Madeline Parker held up her hand to quiet the crowd. "Thank you; thank you so much. And after a wonderful day of enjoying all the rides and the lake, I hope you'll all come out and join me tonight for some music and dancing. Now, I know you're eager to ride the Blue Streak, so let's get on with the show, as we say on Broadway—but I'd like to have some friends of mine give me a hand cutting that ribbon, if it's all right with them. Can I get Mr. Henry Shipley and Miss Ellie Strasbourg to join me?"

I stood up slowly, and with a little push from Father I sheepishly walked to the front of the stage, where I met Ellie.

"Come on, you two," said Madeline. "Don't be shy." She put her arms around us and pointed us at the crowd. "Folks, these two young people were on the train from New York with Alabama and me yesterday, and . . . well, it was quite a trip. I'll leave it at that for now, but trust me, you're going to be hearing more about it real soon. I've spoken to the manager of the park and Mr. Vettel, and we all agree that you two should be the first two riders on the Blue Streak. You'll be in the front seat . . . of the first car . . . on the very first ride! How does that sound? Now let's cut that ribbon!"

On the short walk from the stage to the Blue Streak's loading platform, I'm quite certain that my feet did not touch the ground; I floated on air.

"Can you believe it?" said Ellie as we slid into our seat. "The first ones *ever*. We'll probably be in history books and everything."

I looked doubtfully at her as a photographer from the *Erie Daily Times* pointed his camera at us. "Smile, kids!"

"How does it feel to be a celebrity?" asked Phyllis Finkleman, still scribbling in her notebook and not really listening to our answers. Her eyes were glued to Madeline Parker and Alabama Woodward.

The seat directly behind us was reserved for Sally and Thomas, the two former students from Judge Ambrose's school. They climbed in without saying a word.

I leaned over and whispered to Ellie, "I think those two people from the judge's school are *really* scared."

"Maybe they've never been on a roller coaster before," Ellie said. "Aren't you scared—just a teensy little bit?"

"No," I said firmly. I wasn't lying. I couldn't wait for the ride to begin.

All the remaining seats for the first ride were filled with local kids, the winners of a "Why I Want to Ride the Blue Streak" essay contest sponsored by the park, and when we were all secured in our seats, the ride operator shouted, "All aboard!" which made me think of Clarence and Sam.

Ellie noticed that the smile had disappeared from my face. "Are you sure you're not afraid?"

I scoffed. "No, I was just thinking . . . never mind."

Our heads jerked back as the Blue Streak came to life beneath us, and a cheer rose up from the crowd, which had formed a line that stretched far into the distance. Slowly at first, then gradually building up speed, we slipped into a pitch-black tunnel leading to the steep incline that would take us nearly a hundred feet into the air.

As we rumbled along in the dark, the kids in the back seats screamed.

Suddenly I felt a hand on my shoulder. At first I thought it was Ellie, but I soon realized it couldn't be her; there was just enough light for me to see that both of her hands gripped the bar in front of her.

"Hiya, kids," said a pair of familiar voices.

I spun around and got my first good look at Sally and Thomas, the former students of Judge Ambrose's school. Well, that's who I *expected* to see, anyway. What I *actually* saw, however, sent a chill up my spine. The wigs and fake mustache may have fooled everyone else, but there was no doubt in my mind that I was face to face with my old friends Connie and Ty.

"Good to see you again," said Ty, grabbing me firmly by the arms. A second later, Connie did the same to Ellie, who screamed so loud that it hurt my ears.

"That's okay; scream all you want," said Connie with an evil laugh. "Everyone's expecting it."

The kids behind us took Ellie's scream as a cue and added more of their own.

"You didn't really think you'd seen the last of us, did you?" Connie asked as we twisted and turned through the tunnel. "Do you have *any* idea how much time and effort went into planning that heist? Weeks. *Months.* We had every angle covered. We knew what train you'd be on and which compartment you'd be in. We knew your rich little mommy would have the jewels with her, even what color bag they would be in. It was foolproof."

"But then Dick Tracy Jr. came along and threw a monkey wrench into the works," said Ty, squeezing my arms even harder. "And we can't let you get away with that. What kind of criminals would we be if we did? Huh? Huh?"

"Even dumber than I thought," I said, not quite loud enough for Ty to hear.

"I thought you were in jail," said Ellie.

Connie laughed again. "Sometimes it helps to know people in high places. You kids are pretty smart, but you weren't quite clever enough to figure out that the famous, respectable Judge Ambrose, who taught me everything I know, . . . is my daddy. We didn't even make it to the jail in Erie before we were free. Daddy told them it was all just a misunderstanding, and here we are. In fact, we were probably here before you!"

We were approaching the end of the tunnel, and even after just a few seconds in the darkness, the light was so bright that I had to blink a few times in order to focus.

As we started up the hill, I fought to get loose from Ty's grip, but with only one good hand, it was useless. "What are you going to do to us?" I asked.

"You like rides, right? We're going to give you the ride of your life," said Connie. "Don't worry; we'll wait until we're going really fast, so it'll be *lots* of fun for you. According to Mr. Vettel, we'll hit sixty at the bottom of the first hill. Wheeee!"

"You're going to . . . throw us off?" said Ellie. "That's murder!"

Clackety-clackety-clack went the cars of the Blue Streak as we rose higher and higher.

"Funny, the way I remember it was that you two were showing off for all those kids in the back, and then . . .

whoosh! Me and, uh, Sally Oatley here tried to help you, but it was too late."

"You'll never get away with this," I said, still twisting and turning in Ty's hands. He wasn't about to let me go.

I looked at Ellie. "Whatever you do, don't let go of that bar."

"I won't," she promised. She glanced at my cast. "What about you?"

"I'll be all right."

The steepness of the track pushed me against the seat, making it harder and harder to fight back. As we approached the highest point on the track, the car slowed dramatically, like an out-of-breath climber struggling to reach the summit of one of those mountains in faraway places with names like Katmandu or Tanganyika. A quick glance over the side made me dizzy; it was a long, long way down. I needed a plan, and I needed it *fast*.

Clackety . . . clackety . . . clack-e-ty, and we leveled off, nearly stopping as the cars behind us caught up. And then . . .

Down, down, down we plunged as gravity took over, pulling our car toward the earth at sixty miles per hour and slamming my head back against the seat. Fortunately for us, Connie and Ty were completely caught off guard by the suddenness and the violence of the acceleration, and they lost their grips on Ellie and me for a few seconds as they were flung back into their seats.

Unfortunately, however, there was nowhere for us to go—and besides, we were pinned into our own seats by gravity. We hit the bottom of the first hill and immediately started flying up the two "camelback" hills, when Connie and Ty recovered enough to come after us again. As the kids in the back cars all screamed in unison, completely unaware of what was going on in front of them, our enemies pulled themselves toward us, clutching and grabbing at our flailing arms.

To my horror, even though Ellie screamed, punched, scratched, and bit at her arms, Connie somehow managed to hold on and began to pull Ellie out of her seat. I had no choice but to give up my own fight with Ty and wrap my arms, cast and all, around Ellie's legs, doing everything I could to keep her in our car as we roared down the second hill.

Ty was better prepared for that one, and he used the situation to his advantage, getting his arms around me and his hands locked together. Grunting loud enough to be heard over the clanking of the wheels and the screaming of the kids in the cars at the back, he yanked me completely out of my seat as I continued to hold on to Ellie. As he dragged us both over the back of our seat and on top of him, I kicked and twisted, trying to break free, but instead found my-self with my legs and feet hanging over the side of the car, which was still speeding around the track and climbing the third hill.

When Ty saw that I was already halfway out of the car, he stopped pulling and started pushing me over the edge. "Let the girl go!" he shouted to Connie. "I've got them both!"

I looked up just in time to watch the blood-red scarf that had been tied around Connie's hair flap violently and flut-ter away on the wind. She tried to let go of Ellie, but once again she underestimated the determination of a ten-year-old who was tired of being pushed around. Ellie threw her arms around Connie and held on for dear life.

"Help!" I screamed, panicking as I felt myself slipping backward toward the tracks and the ground far below. Connie's scarf caught my eye again—its rippled red silk looking exactly like a puddle of blood.

The Blue Streak is known as an "out and back" roller coaster. After the first set of hills (the "out" part of the ride), the track takes a hard, 180-degree right-hand turn and heads back to the starting point. The "out" and the "back" parts of the ride are side by side much of the way around, and as I looked farther down the track while still strug-gling to find something—anything—to hang on to, I saw something . . . well, to call it unexpected is just too much of an understatement: it was simply unbelievable.

Running—no, *sprinting*—toward me along the wooden railing that separated the out and back sections was Lantern Sam, who hadn't used up all nine of his lives after all!

The sound of his voice inside my head convinced me that I wasn't seeing things.

"Hang on, kid!" he shouted. Timing his leap perfectly, he then launched himself as if from a catapult at the cars of the Blue Streak, which began plummeting downhill again at more than fifty miles an hour.

And for the second time in as many days, poor, dumb Ty looked up just as seventeen razor-sharp claws and the needle-like teeth of a demented, screeching feline soared through the air, aimed right at his head.

"What the—" Ty yelled. He threw up an arm to shield his face, but it was too late. When you're going sixty miles per hour and you collide head-on with the business end of a ten-pound cat who is flying through the air at twenty-five miles per hour, the results are *not* pretty.

Screaming in pain as Sam dug into him yet again, Ty was forced to let me go, and I pulled myself back into the car just as we reached the bottom of the third hill. The four of us, plus Sam, already packed like sardines in a seat built for two, were slammed against the left side of the car as we raced around the long banked turn that began the return part of the ride. With Ellie still plastered against her, Connie tried to help Ty by swatting at Sam, but the harder she hit him, the more his fur flew and the deeper his claws sunk into her helpless partner and the louder *he* screamed.

"Who *is* that cat?" Connie cried, her face covered in cat hair. "Aaa-chooo!"

Finally, we came out of the turn, the line of cars behind us straightening out as we headed into the long stretch of smaller ups and downs leading back to the starting point. Ty was up on his feet, pulling at Sam, when I spotted a large bucket (left behind by the painters who were still at work painting the miles of lumber that supported the Blue Streak) directly ahead of us and hanging only seven or eight feet above the tracks!

"Sam!" I shouted. "Look out!"

He spun his head around just in time. *"Mrrraa!"*

Instead of jumping down into the car from Ty's shoulders, though, he leaped *up,* groping wildly for the rope and tipping the bucket over in the process. In an instant, gallons of whitewash poured over Ty's head and then spilled onto Connie, Ellie, and me—and then it just kept on coming, coating all those screaming kids in the back cars! I turned around in time to see Sam dangling from the bucket, and I swear this part is true: Lantern Sam was smiling from ear to tattered ear.

In the meantime, the Blue Streak barreled over the last couple of bumps, gradually slowing as we pulled into the loading area with the front seats empty and the four of us still crammed—and dripping with whitewash—into the second row. The crowd, cheering enthusiastically as we came into sight, turned strangely silent when we got closer.

A million shouted questions hit us almost as suddenly as the paint had, but Ellie and I ignored them and jumped out of the car and onto the loading platform.

Ellie pointed at Connie and Ty—beaten, bloodied, and soaked through with paint—and announced, "They tried to kill us!"

"Aaa-chooo!" said Connie.

Mr. Strasbourg and my father, along with a number of other men, moved in and grabbed Connie and Ty, who were too defeated—again—to put up much of a fight.

"Don't let him go!" I said, pointing at Judge Ambrose, who was trying to sneak away. "He's part of it."

Two uniformed policemen blocked his way, and the judge turned back to face us, a resigned look on his face.

The master of ceremonies, still in his Uncle Sam suit, ran up to us, pointing at Connie and Ty. "Who are these two?" he asked. "One of our employees just found Thomas Stapleton and Sally Oatley tied up in a shed."

"They're Connie and Ty," said Ellie. "And they're wanted by the FBI. Judge Ambrose is her *father*. He planned the whole thing. He's nothing but a big crook."

"That's right," I said. "We caught them on the train last night, but then *he* let them go. He was mad because we spoiled his plan to steal the Blue Streak, so he sent them out to kill us. And they almost did, but then . . ."

Every eye in the crowd was on me. Should I tell the truth—that Lantern Sam was the reason Ellie and I were still alive—or should I tell them a story that they would actually believe?

"They were trying to throw us off the roller coaster, but when Ty stood up, he hit his head on a paint bucket." I paused, checking the faces around me, and decided that they all believed me. "And, uh, that's about it."

Then there was lots of handshaking (there would have been hugs, but I was still covered in whitewash) and congratulating, and finally the master of ceremonies convinced everyone that it was time to clean up the Blue Streak and give everyone in the crowd a chance to go for the ride of their lives.

"How about you, Henry?" he asked. "Another ride?"

I couldn't believe that I was saying it, but I smiled and said, "No, thank you. I think I've had enough for one day."

"That was perfect, kid," said a voice inside my head.

"Sam?" I said aloud. Luckily, no one seemed to hear. I searched the area but didn't see him.

"Behind you," he said. *"In the tree."*

He was stretched out along a branch of an elm tree, and I took a few steps toward him. "I thought you didn't like trees."

"I don't. But I wanted a good seat to see how you were going to handle everything. You did great, by the way. Kept my name out of it."

"You have to answer one question," I said. "Last night. The Shoreliner. That bridge. The gorge. I *saw* you. . . ."

"Was there a question in there?" Sam asked, his green eyes twinkling.

"What happened?"

"I must have counted wrong," he said. *"All that time, thinking I'd used up eight lives when obviously that wasn't the case. That time in the barn, when I was just a kitten . . . I guess that one didn't count. Or maybe it was the time with the lantern. When you get right down to it, how do you know which ones count? Take last night, for instance. Does it count? Sure, from your point of view, it looks like it, but it wasn't really so bad. When I went through that door, I'll admit it: for a few seconds, I thought I was a goner. I skipped along the*

edge of the tracks and then went right over the side of the bridge. There was nothing but air between me and the creek and all those pointy rocks. Or so I thought. Lucky for me, they were doing some work on the bridge up near the tracks, and the workers had safety nets in place, just like at the circus. The wind must have blown me back under the bridge, because I hit one of the nets dead center. I bounced around a bit before finally coming to a stop. Then I crawled back up to the tracks and waited for the next train to come along, which I hopped."

"But how did you get *here* from Erie? It must be forty miles!"

"Simple. The Bessemer and Lake Erie line runs straight here from Erie. I hitched a ride on the caboose with Charlie, Clarence's brother, and got here just in time to see you and Ellie disappear into that tunnel at the beginning of the ride. I could barely catch my breath, because the next thing I see is Connie and Ty turning around to wave at Judge Ambrose. And you know the rest."

"All except one thing. I didn't put it all together until just now. Right before you went flying out the door, you tried to tell me that Judge Ambrose was Connie's father, didn't you? How did you know?"

"Ah, that. It was simple. Something the judge said way back when he came after me with that cane. He said that he and his daughter were allergic to cats. At the time I didn't think anything of it. Never thought that she could be on the train. It wasn't until later that it *made sense to me, when I saw how he looked at her. It was the look of a proud father. Now come here—I have something for you."*

I looked around to see if anyone was watching and then slipped quietly over to the tree. "What is it, sardines?" I asked.

"As if I would share my sardines, you silly human. No, what I have isn't quite so valuable . . . to me, that is."

He climbed down from the branch and I dropped down to my knees to pet him. I couldn't help noticing all his scars and that kinked tail and wondering just how many more lives remained in his sorry-looking body.

"Here, give me a hand with this collar," he said, using one of his back legs to push it over his ears.

"You don't wear a collar," I said, feeling for the buckle. My eyes bugged out of my head when I saw that his "collar" was, in fact, Mrs. Strasbourg's necklace, with the Blue Streak sparkling as bright as ever.

"Not bad for a calico from the wrong side of the tracks, eh?" he said.

"How did you . . . but I saw . . . this is impossible," I said, although the very presence of the necklace made it clear that obviously it was *not*.

"I'm surprised at you, kid. I figured that after all we've been through, I wouldn't be able to shock you anymore."

"Well, yeah, but . . . this is *huge*," I said, admiring the necklace in the sunlight.

"*Don't get too attached to that thing,*" said Sam. "*You have to give it back, you know.*"

"I know. It's just . . . I've never seen anything like it. Probably never will again."

"*Oh, I wouldn't be too sure of that. Something tells me that Henry Shipley is going to do very well for himself. I told Clarence, 'We haven't heard the last of that Shipley kid.' And now that I've done all I can do here, it's time I was on my way. I'll catch the Shoreliner on its way back to New York tonight.*"

"Clarence will be surprised to see you," I said. "Won't he?"

"*Not sure anything I do really surprises the old boy anymore. I might get a raised eyebrow out of him when he sees me waiting on the platform, but that'll be about it. It might call for a celebration, though. Sardines, perhaps, especially if I can lay my paws on some of the Sail On brand. You really should try them. They're far superior to the others. They use a higher-quality oil, I think. But I'm boring you. You need to go back to your family, and deliver your little package to Ellie.*"

"Thanks, Sam. I—I . . ."

"*Don't get all sentimental on me, kid, okay? Because if there's one thing I hate—well, besides running out of sardines—it's a long,*" *awkward goodbye scene. I already told you, I haven't heard the last of Henry Shipley. And I'm never wrong."*

And with that, he turned and sauntered away, his tail stubbornly pointing to the left as always.

The party at the Dreamland Ballroom lasted until past midnight (*well* beyond my usual bedtime), but my parents didn't seem to mind that I was still up. With Jessica in Julia's capable hands, they stayed out on the dance floor for hours, making up for the time they'd spent apart while Father was away on the *Point Pelee*. It was the first time I'd ever seen them dance, and I was surprised that they even knew *how*. (Mother told me later that when she and Father first met in 1925, they went dancing almost every Friday night.) I don't think they ever looked happier.

Ellie's mom wore the Blue Streak, which sparkled and shimmered under the spotlights as she and Mr. Strasbourg spun around the floor again and again, like a king and queen in a fairy tale. Ellie ran out of steam before me, falling asleep in her chair, still clutching the stuffed calico cat that her father had won for her on the midway.

Through it all, Madeline Parker belted out song after song in a voice that was used to filling Broadway theaters. At the rear of the ballroom, the enthusiastic young clerk from the hotel desk swayed back and forth in time with the music, eyes closed, a happy, contented look on his face.

Across the room at the bar, however, was the strangest sight of all: Alabama Woodward and a hatless Phyllis Finkleman sharing a table . . . and more than a couple of drinks. Ellie and I had been fully prepared for fireworks when she first asked to join him, but they never came. He actually smiled at her and motioned for her to sit. They even danced a couple of times.

It was that kind of night.

Over breakfast in the hotel dining room, the Strasbourgs offered to drive us home to Ashtabula, but Father declined, insisting that they had already done too much for us.

"Nonsense," said Mrs. Strasbourg. "We'll be in debt to Henry for the rest of our lives. At the very least, you must permit us to have Billings drop you off at the train station."

"That would be much appreciated," said Father.

Outside, under a blazing morning sun, Mr. Strasbourg shook my hand once more, and Mrs. Strasbourg hugged me, squeezing the breath out of me. "Thank you, Henry. Thank you, thank you, thank you."

Even though she'd only known me for a couple of days, Ellie knew there was no chance I was going to hug her. She walked up to me and stuck out her hand, very businesslike.

"It was a pleasure meeting you, Henry Shipley," she said with just a hint of a smile.

"Um ... yeah ... me too," I said, shaking her hand. "Maybe we'll ... um ..."

"Of course we will," she said. "I already told you, we're going to be friends forever."

I climbed into the backseat of the car, closed my eyes, and took a deep breath. A voice calling my name made me look up one last time as Billings turned the car toward the exit. It was Ellie, of course.

"Henry! I kept something of yours! I'm sorry!" she shouted. But judging by the size of the grin on her face, she wasn't sorry at all.

"What is she talking about?" I wondered aloud. "She's such a ... girl."

Billings pulled the car out into the street and accelerated away from the amusement park.

It took me about ten seconds more to realize what she'd kept: my sketchbook. It had my name and address inside, and I knew for certain that (to borrow a phrase from Lantern Sam) I hadn't heard the last of Ellie Strasbourg.

School let out for summer vacation a few days later. There's nothing quite like those first days of freedom after nine endless months of grammar and geography and uncomfortable clothes. My parents had given me a break from my usual summer chores because of my cast, so I wandered down to the pier where the *Point Pelee* was docked and spent some time watching the crew, who were hanging over the side, touch up her paint before her next voyage. Even though the *Point Pelee* was "past her prime," Father was very particular about the way she looked.

When that grew old, I decided to go to the train station, hoping to catch a glimpse of the Shoreliner as it stopped in Ashtabula on its way back to New York. My timing was perfect; as I stepped onto the platform, I heard a train's horn in the distance and looked down the tracks.

"Do you know what train that is?" I asked the man selling newspapers.

"That'll be the Shoreliner," he said without looking up. "Right on time."

I felt a grin spread across my face as the big locomotive went past, its wheels gripping the iron rails as it slowed to a stop at the far end of the platform.

"Ashtabula!" called out a familiar voice. "Ashtabula, this stop!" Clarence stepped down from the car to the platform and checked his pocket watch. I smiled, remembering how many times I'd seen him do that.

"You're late!" I shouted.

He hesitated, frowning and checking his watch again.

Suddenly he looked up and spotted me. "Henry! Thank goodness you're here!"

Behind him, Sam leaped onto the platform and raced toward me. For a moment I thought he was in a hurry just to see me. I should have known better.

"C'mon, kid, we have to work fast. That ship of your father's—it's called the Point Pelee, right?"

"Yeah. Why?"

"Is it still in port?"

"Yes. What's going on?"

"It's those wacky Henshaw Sisters—Gladys and Gwendolyn! Remember, the ones who sing like a couple of dogs howling at the moon?"

"Of course I remember. What about them?"

"They have a brother named George, and we have to find him quicker than you can say 'canned sardines.' For the past eleven months and three weeks, those crazy dames have turned every port on the Great Lakes upside down looking for Georgie-boy. If they don't get his John Hancock on some important papers in the next seven days, they're going to lose their business. I know, I know—normally when I hear a story like that, I shrug and say something sarcastic and snide, but this time it's different."

"Why?" I asked suspiciously.

"Sardines, kid. Millions of them. A lifetime supply."

I glanced at Clarence. "What is he talking about?"

"He's telling the truth," said Clarence. "Apparently, the Henshaws own a sardine cannery out in California, but they owe some back taxes on the property. There's another piece of property they're trying to sell to raise the money, but all three of the Henshaw kids' names are on the deed. They can't sell without George's signature."

"What does any of this have to do with the *Point Pelee*?" I asked.

Sam sighed. *"That's what I've been trying to tell you. Gladys and Gwendolyn have been searching for their brother for a year, and a few days ago they met somebody in Duluth, Minnesota, who informed them that George is the cook aboard the Point Pelee. Small world, eh, kid?"*

"Holy Catawba! George! I *know* him! He's the one who saves the sardine keys for me! I guess that explains why they have so many sardines on board. Uh-oh. What time is it?" I asked, suddenly remembering the promise I'd made to Father to wave to him from the jetty.

"One-eighteen," said Clarence. "On the nose." The train shuddered to life behind him.

"The *Point Pelee* casts off at three-thirty! And then they won't be in port for *days*."

"I'm waiting on you," said Sam. *"As usual."*

Clarence tipped his cap at me as he stepped aboard the Shoreliner, already in motion. "Take care of Sam for me, Henry. He's living on borrowed time."

I saluted him. "Yes, sir. I'll get him back to you in one piece, I promise."

"Let's go get him, kid," said Lantern Sam as the Shoreliner faded into the distance.

Epilogue
February 2012

As I turned into the driveway, I read the name that had been stenciled on the mailbox and smiled at my wife. A storybook-perfect farmhouse stood before us, and on a slight rise behind it sat a small barn, its red sides glowing against the dull gray sky. In the backseat, my great-grandson Kevin stared out the rain-streaked side window of the station wagon and sighed loudly.

"Where are we? Who are the Nockwoods?"

"We're in a town called Dunkirk. Carl Nockwood is a friend. I met his grandfather, Clarence, back in 1938 when I was about your age. He was the conductor on the Lake Erie Shoreliner, a very famous train."

"What are we doing here, anyway?"

"We're picking up a kitten. And visiting old friends."

"A *kitten?* We drove two hours to pick up a *kitten?* There are kittens in Pittsburgh, you know."

"This is not just any kitten," I said, turning off the engine and glancing at him in the rearview mirror. "This is a very special cat."

"One in a million," said my wife with a wink in my direction.

"It's turning to snow," Kevin said, opening his door. "Grrreeeaaat. My sneakers will be ruined."

"Don't you want to know why he's special?" I asked, resisting the temptation to remind him that I had told him to wear boots.

"Not really," said Kevin. He must have realized how rude he sounded, because he tried to act interested as we trudged along the slushy path to the barn. "Okay, what's so special about it? Is it like a show cat or something?"

"No, nothing like that. Do you know what a calico is?"

"I've heard of it. But no. I guess not."

"Calicoes have three colors: black, white, and orange. They're quite common; you've seen a million of them. What you probably *didn't* know is that there's something special about them. They're almost always female. If you want to know why, you could look it up on that computer of yours;

it's all about genes and chromosomes and the sort of thing you learn about in school. But notice that I said *almost* always. That's because every once in a great while, when the sun and the moon and the stars are in the right spots at exactly the right time, something very special occurs: a male calico. Clarence was fond of saying that it was a one in a million chance, but he had a habit of exaggerating. It's really more like one out of every three thousand calicoes." I opened the barn door and we all stepped inside.

I waved at Carl, who was feeding some calves at the far end of the barn.

"Be with you in a minute!" he shouted.

Kevin tugged on my sleeve. "Is that why we're here? Are you getting a male calico?"

I nodded, and he actually smiled; it was his first of the day. "Cool."

"He's not just any male calico, either, you see. This kitten also *happens* to be related to a very special cat—a cat I met when I was exactly your age. His name is Lantern Sam."

"*Was.*"

"Sorry?"

"You said, 'His name *is* Lantern Sam.' I think you meant to say *was.*"

"Oh, right," I said. "Of course. It was all a very long time ago. Seventy-four years this May. Seems hard to believe. *Tempus fugit.*"

Clarence's grandson Carl joined us, and after the usual greetings, he led us to the stall where the mother cat, a mostly white calico, cared for her five kittens.

"This one's the boy," said Carl, lifting and handing me a miniature version of Sam, minus all the scars and missing ear parts. The patch over his eye and the lantern-shaped spot on his side matched Sam's almost exactly.

"Remarkable," noted my wife.

"Spitting image," I said.

"Yessir," Carl said with a chuckle. "I never met the original, but I've seen the pictures of Lantern Sam, of course. Kind of famous in these parts. If you stuck your nose in every barn in town, you'd probably find one of Sam's descendants in almost all of them. I don't think anybody knows how many generations it's been, but once every ten or fifteen years, a boy pops up and everybody makes a big fuss. Last one was back in ninety-nine, just up the road. Little girl got her picture in the paper with him. As soon as I saw this furry fellow, I knew I had to call you two. I think Gramps would have come back to haunt me if I hadn't."

"I—we—appreciate that," I said. "When do you think we can take him home?"

"He's six weeks now. Let's give him another four or five weeks. How does that sound?"

"Perfect. Let's make it March 15."

"The Ides of March," said my wife. "Sam would have appreciated that. He did love his Shakespeare."

"What?" said Kevin. "You're kidding, right?"

Carl caught my eye. "You haven't told him?"

"No, not yet," I said. "I've been waiting for . . . the right time."

"The right time for *what*?" Kevin asked. "What didn't you tell me?"

I set the kitten in the straw with his siblings. "We'll be back for you real soon, little fellow. That'll give us time to come up with a proper name."

"Grandpa! Grandma! What is going on?"

"Oh! Almost forgot!" I said, reaching into my coat pocket. "I have something for him! Sail On sardines. These were always—"

"Mrrraaa," came the voice of an unseen cat, hiding somewhere near the back of the barn.

I craned my neck and caught the briefest of glimpses of a calico as it slipped through a narrow opening in the wall. A *very* narrow opening. Now, I'm not saying that this means anything, and I'm not a hundred percent certain, but it seemed to me that the top half of that cat's tail had a *definite* left-hand bend.

"Everything okay?" asked Carl. "You look like you've seen a ghost."

"What's that? Oh, yes. Everything's just perfect. Now, as I was saying, these were always Sam's favorite. He always insisted that they had the *perfect* amount of oil. And salt. Just the right balance. Wish I had a nickel for every time he said *that*."

Kevin bounced up and down, growing more and more impatient. "*Who* said?"

I ignored him and handed the sardines to Carl. "Thanks again for calling us. We'll see you in a few weeks. Let me know what he thinks of the sardines. Something tells me that he won't be shy. If he doesn't like them, you're going to hear about it."

"Wh-what?" cried Kevin. "Did I miss something?"

My wife took him by the arm and led him toward the car. "I think it's time we told you a little story. What do you think, Henry?"

"I think you're right as usual, Ellie."

Don't Call Me Samantha
THE ALMOST ENTIRELY TRUE
AUTOBIOGRAPHY OF LANTERN SAM

Final Thoughts of the Deepest Kind

All right. By now you have figured out that I didn't die when I went flying out the door of the Shoreliner as it crossed the Chautauqua Creek Bridge.

Or the time I was squashed by a cow.

Or when I was skewered by an arrow.

Or chucked overboard into Lake Erie.

Or even when a rooster with anger-management issues thrashed me, forcing me to leap from a moving pickup truck onto the street, where I was promptly flushed down a sewer drain and into Lake Erie (again).

Or the time that I, sleeping soundly, plummeted fifty feet from a treetop and landed on a Chihuahua.

Or when I was very nearly decapitated by a cleaver-throwing cook.

Or incinerated by a railroad lantern and then turned into an ice sculpture.

Or even the time I was trapped between the Hound of the Baskervilles and the 5:15 from Akron.

Now, I don't know about you, but when *I* read that list, I count nine lives. But here I am—breathing, eating, drinking, stockpiling sardines—doing all those normal cat activities, plus a few of the not-so-normal variety, such as solving crimes and writing an autobiography. I suppose there's a reasonable explanation. Perhaps some of my misadventures were just bad days—not the kind I would ever want to repeat, but maybe not quite worth a whole *life*. Take, for example, my first dip in Lake Erie, courtesy of the captain of the *Susie* G. Yes, I was a few miles offshore, and yes, the lake was rough that day, but I knew how to swim and, sooner or later, I would have made it back to shore. So maybe that one doesn't count.

I guess the real question is: How many of those nine lives *have* I used up? And how will I ever know the answer?

Look, here's what I think: Two lives, or five, or nine? What's the difference when you get down to the nitty-gritty? Because the truth is, whether you're a cat like me or some being of lesser intelligence, it's not the number of lives that's important; it's what we *do* with the time we're given that really matters. Take it from someone who has been through the wringer a few times: I know what counts most in life, and it's the simple things. Family. Good friends. A warm bed. Fresh milk. And, of course, quality sardines.

My philosophy of life, which, I'll admit, I borrowed from a shampoo bottle, goes something like this: Carpe diem. Sleep. Repeat.

And don't ever stop.

A Note to the Reader

Although the Lake Erie Shoreliner is a fictional train, the Blue Streak, in Conneaut Lake, Pennsylvania, is very real, and celebrated its seventy-fifth-anniversary season in 2013. In 1993, the American Coaster Enthusiasts recognized it as an ACE Coaster Classic—one of the first roller coasters to be so named. They further granted it a Coaster Landmark Award, honoring historically significant roller coasters, in 2010.

MICHAEL D. BEIL is the author of the Edgar Allan Poe Award–nominated Red Blazer Girls mystery series, as well as the stand-alone middle-grade novel *Summer at Forsaken Lake*.

Mr. Beil, who teaches English, spent his childhood with his nose planted firmly in copies of Encyclopedia Brown and Sherlock Holmes. He didn't like lending books to friends because he was afraid he'd never get them back. This is still true today.

He and his wife, Laura Grimmer, live in Manhattan and Connecticut with two dogs and two cats (who may or may not be descended from Lantern Sam). For more on the author and his books, visit him online at michaeldbeil.com.